Angry Archie Thrasher
and the Others

J. Michael Wilhelm

Goose River Press
Waldoboro, Maine

Library of Congress Card Number: 2022934041

ISBN: 978-1-59713-245-9

First Printing, 2022

.

Published by
Goose River Press
3400 Friendship Road
Waldoboro ME 04572
e-mail: gooseriverpress@gmail.com
www.gooseriverpress.com

CONTENTS

For Donna with love

John Dee

An Englishman, Dr. John Dee,
When Elizabeth l was queen,
With his scryver's help
Looked into the yelp
And yaw at what could not be seen—

The blessing and bark of angels,
The sway of the constellations—
To explain the unknowns
And the magical zones
Of mystical revelation.

Does the earth encircle the sun?
A blasphemous question for some.
But not for John Dee
For whom such beliefs
Were the spark of fascination.

The smartest man on earth, some said,
Most knowledgeable and well-read,
His library famed,
His writings acclaimed
Were assets and also grave threats.

Astrology and astronomy,
Alchemy and cryptography,
Crystals and charts,
Maps of the stars,
The language of Adam and Eve,

Led Dee to describe gravity
Before Isaac Newton's theory;
That unequal weights
Fall at the same rate
Before Galileo's query.

All such rich food for deep thought
Where the mind might get led and caught,
A reformation
Of speculation
The queen so eagerly sought.

John Dee became her advisor
As she straddled a world divided
'Tween papist dogma
And protestant thought
In which fear and hope resided.

What was this man's legacy?
Instead of fame, sad infamy.
Deluded mystic,
Obsessed eccentric
Lost to accepted history.

Elliot

I was sitting at the bar on Newbury Street, indulging in my usual TGIF drink on my way home from work when he approached me from the side. "Schultzy," he said, "what a surprise!" He put his hand on my shoulder. I didn't recognize him. "What are you doing in the city?" he asked.

I looked up at him, searching his face for a recognizable feature, but nothing about it recalled a name. My first reaction was to pretend that I knew him and answer the question, but his tone was so annoying that I responded in kind."I'm sorry, do I know you?" I asked.

"Sure, you do. I'm Elliot, you know, your fellow alum from MIT."

"Oh," I said. "We were in school together?"

He took the back of the seat next to me, twisting the bar stool toward me, sat down, put an elbow on the bar, his face in his hand, looked at me and said, "You look great, buddy."

"Really? I don't remember you."

"Oh, right, why would you remember me? I'm sorry."

The bartender stood in front of him waiting for his order. "I'll have whatever he's having. Looks like a Heinekens."

I was surprised. How could he know my draft was a Heinekens just by looking at the beer in the glass?

"We were in the same class," he continued, "but I don't think we ever really crossed paths. Your picture is in the year book. Schultz Bogdanovic. Right there between Theresa Bickford and Boxer Brogan. Remember her? The one with the blue hair before it was fashionable?"

"You know, I don't," I said. "There were like a thousand students in our class."

"One thousand one hundred and forty-five to be exact," he reported in an off-handed way.

I took a moment to look at him more closely, thinking that there was an outside chance we had been in the same course at some point. His pale blue oxford shirt was overwhelmed by his protruding stomach that spilled over his belt. His thighs stretched his khaki pants. What little hair remained on his head was barely noticeable and his head bobbed as he talked, as if he was nodding affirmatively to a question that hadn't been asked. A round face with gray eyes completed a picture that meant nothing to me.

"You know, it's funny but I've been thinking about you of late," he continued. "I predicted, to myself of course, that I'd bump into you. And here you are and here I am. How about that!"

I was skeptical. "I don't get it," I said. "Why would you be thinking about me? We don't know each other."

"Because I saw you in the crystals about a month ago. There you were walking across campus. You were with a tall thin woman with beautiful long blonde hair."

"Emily," I said, incredulous. "My good friend Emily Weiss?"

"Yes. Emily Weiss. She was in the class just behind yours. Had an apartment near the Coop."

I could feel myself getting tense. How did he know all this? Where did this guy come from? Was he for real? Was this some kind of set up? And if so, for what? I thought he was about to express some sympathy for Emily's death a year after her graduation. Instead he abruptly changed the subject. "So, you're in the data business now, I hear," he said in that confident tone of his.

"Yes," I said. "I analyze data from our researchers. We're searching for a cure for Parkinson's."

"That's cute," he replied, "researchers searching and, of course, re-searching because that's what they do."

If it was meant to be a joke, it wasn't funny. "This is serious work," I said. "We may someday find a cure for a debilitating illness. But you must already know what I do from those crystals, right?"

"Are you making fun of me?" he asked.

"No, I'm serious. What the hell does it mean when you say you saw me in the crystals?"

"You've heard of Merlin and the crystal cave, I assume," he answered. "You've heard that crystals emanate energy. You know that psychics interact with crystals like fluorite and amethyst to enhance their powers, that crystals have been used for centuries to heal and to communicate with the past and the future. I know you know all this. Why pretend you don't?"

He was right. I did know all this. Crystals had been a project of mine for a science class in high school my sophomore year, a topic suggested by my teacher, Mrs. Watson, a woman with intense energy and with a captivating excitement for her subject. It was she who urged me to apply to MIT. My project was "substandard" she had said. I couldn't get excited about the topic. I wasn't convinced.

"Schultzy, let me buy you another beer. I'm here as your friend. By the way, I like the look: the bow tie, the wire rimmed glasses and the goatee. Reminds me of Freud or was it Nietzsche? I don't know. Here's the thing: I want you to help me. We can make a lot of money together. You've got skills that complement mine. That taken together they could prove very profitable." He waved the bartender over and ordered.

"So, what skills do you have?" I asked.

"With those crystals I can conjure the voices of the dead futurists. Kind of an oxymoron, don't you think? Alvin Toffler, Buckminster Fuller, Dandridge Cole, Erich Jantsch. I'm a stock broker. With their help we can know what others don't and invest in future realities before anyone else. Did Andrew Weinreich know the potential of his Six Degrees when he constructed that first viable social network? If he could have looked into the future, imagine what he could have accomplished and the amount of money he would have made."

I was incredulous. "If you believe you can do this, why do you need me?" I asked.

"I need you to help me understand the data, understand what they're telling me. I need someone to triangulate the information to understand where their different opinions actually converge. I don't have the skills for that. I'm a linear thinker."

"Are you telling me that you've already had these conservations? That you've talked to the dead somehow?" Those same uncomfortable feelings I had harbored as a high school student, skeptical of the crystal enthusiasts, resurfaced. I didn't believe them then and I didn't believe him now.

"Yes," he said in a whisper, leaning closer to me. "Yes, I have too much information, too much. I can't get my head around it. They're talking about things like moon colonization and human organ regeneration and cars that fly and artificial food. I don't know where to plant my flag. I can only talk with them one at a time. You know, that's how this crystal power works."

"No, I don't," I said in normal voice to counter the secrecy his whisper suggested. "How does it work?"

"I thought you knew. That high school science project of yours was all about crystals."

"You know about my high school project? What the hell? We're talking high school, man, sophomore year. The year of the wise fool. I read some articles, cut out pictures of crystals, stuck them on some poster board and wrote a summary of what I read. That's it. My teacher wanted me to delve deeper, but I didn't know what that meant. I got a B minus and that was a gift. You're talking to the wrong guy. And by the way, I don't believe you."

"What don't you believe?" he asked sounding disappointed.

"You, I don't believe you. Or any of this!"

"Want to know how I know about that science project?"

"Sure," I said half-heartedly.

"Mrs. Watson told me a few days ago. She recommended you to me. You know she died, right? The year we graduated from MIT.

Mirror Self

When looking at your mirror self
Did you ever think it someone else,
A perfect stranger,
Doppelgänger,
Acknowledging how strange it felt?

Your reflection in a window
Is someone you have never known,
Dressed much like you,
The face askew,
An expression that you'd never show.

And that photo of the family,
In the place where you were standing
A different man,
The awkward stance,
The smirk and pose just maddening.

The evil twin, the second self,
The double that was on the shelf,
To take your place,
To fill your space,
And turn your world upon itself.

Is it real or just a phantom,
Mental prank, paroxysm?
How would you know
It comes and goes,
Each appearance new and random.

You hope that it will disappear.
Slip back into the stratosphere.
This specter from
A mind undone,
The object of some crazy fear

Bob and Rebecca

They were traveling to the village, two retirees off to do their shopping. She was looking out the window as they passed the gun shop. He noticed and it brought back the memory of a previous conversation." "You know," he said, I've been thinking about what you said about getting a gun."

"Not from that place!" Her voice had the sharp edge of disgust.

"No, not from that place," he replied. "What's on his road sign today?"

"I didn't catch it all, something about the dangerous Mexicans and crossing the border. I swear he's a fascist."

"The bane of free speech," he said quietly, as much to himself as to her. They were a short, round couple dressed in their jeans and autumn sweaters who were still getting used to running errands together. Bob and Rebecca Michaud, she a small version of Bette White and he a short heavier Bob Hope. Retirement had given them new-found time to do the house-hold chores together.

"No," he continued, "what I was about to say was that maybe you should get a gun, a small, lightweight hand gun, in case you need to protect yourself. Like a .22 revolver."

"I thought you were dead set against the idea?" Rebecca asked.

"Great choice of words. And yes, I was, but now I'm not so much. We do live on a road with few neighbors." He paused for a moment. "You are alone some evenings when I'm at the vet hall, for example. I'm just saying if it would make you feel safer, if that's what this is about, I want you to feel safe."

A blustery wind blew dry leaves across the road as the sun went behind an array of gray clouds. They were almost to the village and the only grocery store for many miles. "You know that place a few minutes from here that not only sells them, but also has a firing range and lessons? We should talk to them about what gun would be best for you and about lessons."

"Why can't you give me lessons?" she asked. "There can't be that much to it? What? Pull the hammer back and pull the trigger? We can practice in the field. Shucks, we've got ten acres. We can shoot out there to our heart's content without killing anybody."

"Wouldn't you feel better learning from a pro?"

"Hell, no! What do they know that you don't?"

***

He pulled into the parking lot of the grocery store and found a spot near the door. He noted to himself that the other cool thing about retirement was that you could time your errands for your parking convenience. The gun conversation was now officially over. And as was often the case, she had had the last word.

The fact was Bob didn't want to teach her how to use it. His experience had been with military grade weapons, powerful and dangerous instruments meant to kill with an insane precision. He never felt comfortable with them in basic training and, when he ultimately deployed as a unit supply specialist, he never had the occasion to sight a gun at another human being.

Also bothersome was the vibe going through his head about "responsibility." If it did happen that he showed her how to shoot and she actually shot at someone for some reason, it might reflect back on him and the quality of his teaching. He remembered how his dad made him take a gun safety course before he could get his hunting license. He figured it was as much for his dad's safety as his own.

And what if Rebecca was in danger of someone shooting at her and she shot and missed and was shot and killed? Would it have been that his training had failed her? Or what if her aim went awry and she hit some innocent bystander? Or if an intruder only shot her because he saw the gun in her hand? Could he be responsible for that too?

***

Two weeks later they returned home from their errands with a Glock 19. Rebecca had been surprised that small guns cost so much, even though she chose one of the cheaper ones. As Rebecca explained to Bob, she didn't want them spending a lot of money on something she would probably never use. The comment nagged at him all the way home. Given his original reservations, this added yet another. Over time, she might forget how to use it, and when it was needed, would be confused and at risk.

After a few lessons out in the field, the Glock found its way into an open shoe box under their bed. Rebecca felt safe, and Bob forgot his misgivings. For a year or so, every few months, he would suggest gun practice. She took him up on the offer only once. Now, five years later, hidden away, under the bed, the loaded Glock was a forgotten member of the family.

***

When Bob's years of life spilled over 70, he began to notice the subtle changes of aging. His gate was slower. His hearing failed him in noisy rooms. His visits to his opthalmologist had become annual events. And, of course, the ability to recall names and facts became mysteriously elusive.

Retirement had created a void Bob had not been able to fill. He had been assigned the counter of the village post office for over 25 years and he missed the friendly stream of faces at his station, the acquired name recognition of frequent patrons, and the pleasure drawn from answering their questions. He missed Francine at the counter beside him, the funniest person he'd ever known, whose repartee with customers got everyone waiting in line laughing. He even missed the muddy, lukewarm coffee in the back room that he believed was poisonous.

He found himself bored and restless. He had no reason to get out of bed. The old routines were gone, the ones he could count on: going to work, coming home, having a beer, eating dinner, watching the news—the comfort foods of his life. Now as he tried to busy himself around the house, his activities were largely limited to the cycles of seasons beyond its walls—raking leaves, shoveling snow, raking leaves, planting the garden, mowing the lawn, raking leaves.

Even the vet hall had let him down. Most of the older guys, his Vietnam buddies, were gone and Bob had trouble relating to the younger ones.

His one true friend, Avery, would join him for a drink once in a while, but Avery had transformed himself into an energy consultant, found most of his work out of state and was gone for days. Avery and his wife Justine had been their nearest neighbors, a half mile down the road, and had grown close with Bob and Rebecca. But seven years past, Justine had died. Avery sold the house and moved into their camp at the lake. Now, even when Avery was around, he wasn't, as far as Bob was concerned.

***

Bob was surprised when Avery called one night and invited him to meet for drinks at the Sebago Restaurant. It had been almost four months since they had seen each other, and it was "time to get caught up," Avery said. This meant hearing about Avery's latest projects and where he had been, and how cities were deteriorating, and how there was nothing that could compare with life at the lake.

"What about you?" Avery asked after delivering his commentary. "What's going on?"

"Not much," Bob replied, unable to think of anything equally as interesting as Avery's stories.

"Surely something exciting has been happening with you guys. Spill the beans, man."

"You know, I've been working around the house. Built a grape arbor by the back porch, put in a small patio. Rebecca and I went to the Fryeberg Fair last week. Stuff like that."

"Doesn't sound that exiting to me," Avery said, disappointment in his voice.

"It's okay. I haven't worked much with my hands all these years, and its different." Bob wanted to tell him the truth about his state of mind, that he was bored and restless, but didn't want to unload on him.

He didn't have to. Avery heard no enthusiasm in Bob's voice. "Come on Bob, that's not good enough. You've got to change your mind set, you've got to turn your life around, find a hobby, learn a craft, get out and meet people, volunteer. You sound bored to death."

Bob took a sip of his beer and looked around the restaurant. He didn't see anyone he knew who might be listening. Avery responded to the silence. "All I'm saying is you should make an effort to break the monotony. That's what it is Bob, your life has become monotonous and that can be a killer. If anything will bring on dementia, it's thoughtless days."

"I know," Bob admitted.

"So, do something about it. Reinvent yourself. Take a course, join a club, get a hobby, take flying lessons. Become someone else. You could join a theater group. It would keep your mind super active. Think of all the lines you'd have to learn and the blocking and all that. Those companies in

15

Portland always need amateurs to fill small parts"

"You've got to be kidding, Avery," Bob responded, finally animated. "Look at me. I'm short and overweight. Who would want to look at me on stage?"

"So is Danny Devito. Come on, Bob, it was just an example. Just do something for yourself. Get a Harley. Why not? Get a tattoo. Ride the tiger. You just need to figure out which tiger to ride."

Their conservation ended with reminiscing about old times and Avery sharing a few new jokes. Bob drove home unsettled and disappointed in himself. It was like he hadn't upheld his end of a bargain that Avery assumed they'd made, to make the most of these last years. He arrived home to find Rebecca sound asleep in front of the TV. He gently roused her, sent her off to bed, and finished watching Criminal Minds for her.

***

Brushing his teeth preparing for bed, Bob looked at himself in the mirror. He noticed that his beard was growing out like a white rash. He hadn't shaved for a few days, and acknowledged that he'd pretty much given up on the morning ritual and wondered why Rebecca hadn't said anything. Given his thinning white hair, he didn't like the way the beard and hair embraced his face like a bleached towel. "What the hell," he said to himself and grasped the razor to shave it off, then reconsidered. "I'll wait 'til tomorrow," he said to himself.

Even with little to do, this was the way Bob responded to most things recently. If it wasn't urgent, he'd put if off. It was just another symptom of his ennui. When leisure time had been minimal, all tasks required immediate attention. Now they could all wait.

Bob was upset by Avery's assessment of his life, and he couldn't get to sleep. He imagined the various transformations he could attempt and immediately discarded the ones that were inconceivable. Theater was out of the question. Not a single hobby of any kind came to mind. He could go fishing more often, he thought, get a small boat and work on his casting. He saw himself bringing home a string of fish for Rebecca to cook, and then remembered the catch-and-release rule and the admonition to eat only one fish caught in Maine lakes due to the mercury in the water. So much for that idea.

A Harley was out of the question—Rebecca would never allow that—but a tattoo was not. Maybe that would be a place to start the transformation. A retired postal clerk with a bold tattoo, he thought. There was enough asymmetry there to qualify as a tiger rider. And depending on the location of the inked skin, he could ride it as he chose. Same with the beard. Why not grow it out? He could always shave it off. With a decision made, he fell asleep.

***

"How's Avery doing these days?" Rebecca asked at breakfast. "What did you guys talk about last night?"

"Mostly about Avery," Bob answered. "He's pretty busy with his business and had a bunch of new stories to tell."

"That's a good thing," she responded. "He needed something to take his mind off Justine's death. He seemed in fine spirits?"

"He did."

"What about you? What stories did you have to tell?"

"Oh, you know. Going to the Fryeburg Fair, stuff like that. Not quite as interesting as Avery's."

"What are you saying, Bob? I don't like what that implies," she said, clearly irritated with him.

"What do you mean?"

"Would life be more exciting for you if I wasn't around, if you were able to be off living the good life like Avery with nothing to tie you down?" She got up and turned her back to him to look out the kitchen window.

"Of course not. Why would you even say such a thing?"

"Because you sounded disappointed with your life, while there's Avery, free to do whatever he wants."

"I didn't say that."

"It sure sounded like it to me. You should hear yourself. You sound bored to death. And look at you! When was the last time you shaved? You look like a bum."

Bob felt he had to assert himself. "I'm growing a beard," he said, his voice barely audible.

"Great," she said, sarcastically, walking out of the room.

This had to be the moment Bob should tell her about the tattoo. He didn't want another argument in the future. He needed to roll this into one and get it over with. She had taken the stairs to their bedroom and he followed after her.

Making the bed, her back was to him as he walked into the bedroom. This made it easier for him. "Becca," he said softly. "You know I love you. I didn't mean anything like that."

She turned to face him, her soft features fighting off tears, and slowly sat down on the edge of the bed. "This retirement thing hasn't been easy, has it?" she asked rhetorically, almost in a whisper. She patted the bed in an invitation for him to sit beside her. "I want you to be happy, honey. I want us to be happy. It's easy to see that you're not. If there's anything I can do to help, just tell me."

It was like she had let a fresh autumn wind blow through the room, scuttling the dead leaves into its corners, out of the way. Bob sat down beside her and told her about his evening with Avery and the truth of his life as he now understood it. The most he was capable of immediately was the beard and tattoo he said. And all he sought from her was understanding.

***

18

The magazines *Tattoo Energy, Skin Shots, Inked, Tattoo Life,* and *Freshly Inked* covered the dining room table. Rebecca dog-eared each magazine page Bob wanted to remember as he searched for images that appealed to him. Initially he did not discriminate regarding size, body part, or colors. This first run was only to rate the value of his initial reaction. He would have to review them all again, once he determined where he wanted the art displayed. The options seemed endless. In each case he only had the November issue of the magazine. This could take a while, he thought, each month bringing a new array of options, each option a reconsideration of any previous decision.

Rebecca helped him hone the process. If he picked the most appealing tattoo from each magazine, she said, and ranked the five, he'd find what he wanted.

Still, Bob returned every day to the magazines, revisiting each tattoo pictured from cover to cover. Tattoos were permanent and he could not make a mistake.

Then he remembered how much he loved the record album covers from the '60's, '70's and '80's—*Abraxsas, The Dark Side of the Moon, The Inarticulate Speech of the Heart, Disraeli Gears*—the colors, the images, how they reflected the music and how it connected to his life. He was onto something and had an epiphany. The songs themselves spoke to the recent transformation of his state of mind from "Comfortably Numb" to "Be Here Now."

Rebecca suggested that he draw his own. At first, he rejected the idea, acknowledging he lacked the skills. But she urged him to at least try, surprising him with a trove of colored pencils and a couple sketch pads. "What do you want to say?" she asked. "Is there a message you want to send? Who's your audience? Even if it's only yourself, even if it's only seen by you when you look in the mirror, you want it to mean something, don't you? Even the colors you choose will be important."

"You're making this much too complicated," he said, somewhat annoyed. "I can't draw. I'm just looking for something colorful and kind of crazy."

"Crazy how? And how crazy?"

"Didn't you just say the same thing twice?"

"No. I can make a crazy face for you and then make it crazier. Want to see?"

He smiled. "You're great. Putting up with me. Playing along. Giving me these art supplies. I love you. I'll try."

"Good," she said, walking away. "You can use the kitchen table for your easel. It's all yours."

***

The fact was he couldn't draw, and the magazine search proved too overwhelming. "Let's just go to that tattoo place in the village," he suggested, "and see what they would suggest."

With the guidance of Andre the artist at *Tattoo You*, he chose a serpent in blues, greens and reds crawling up his neck from his shoulder. More dramatic than he would have originally considered, but Andre had his assistant take off his shirt to expose a serpent that seemed to move when he shrugged his right shoulder. "Incredible, don't you think? An animated tattoo?" Andre asked with a smile. Bob was sold. "We'll have to shave your neck and trim that side of your beard a bit. Don't want to hide the effect. You've got a good growth growin' there. Looks great."

Bob smiled with pride. The beard was easy, he thought. A natural, painless modification of who he was. In fact, he now believed shaving was a violation of his true self. Likewise, there was something primitive and intimately personal about the tattoo, a return to a time when body painting was a form of identification and spiritual connection.

***

With the beard and tattoo Bob's new appearance caused a reciprocal change in the appearance of others. Friends and acquaintances offered a wry smile on their first meeting with the new Bob. Strangers took more than one look. The tattoo brought an unfamiliar attention to him and was a surprising conversation starter, especially with those similarly inked. At first uncomfortable with this new reality, Bob slowly came to enjoy the notoriety and repartee it inspired. It seemed to replace the friendly banter that he and Francine had enjoyed with their postal patrons.

***

At home he was the same old guy. Rebecca complained some about the beard, noting that he no longer looked like the man she married, but never mentioned the tattoo. He tended to his household chores but found himself leaving for the village more often, running errands, getting sandwiches for lunch, satisfying an urge for a chai from Starbucks or an ice cream from DQ, going to Planet Fitness, unconsciously seeking the new found attention. It was at Planet Fitness that he compared his tattoo with others on display and found himself yearning for more. Why not color his calf with a lightning bolt or his bicep with Rebecca's name. His chest was an empty canvas that begged for something special.

***

Two years later at 74 years old, Bob barely resembled his former self. His face was hidden behind a full beard. His almost daily visits to Planet Fitness had straightened the round body, effectively making him look taller. A second serpent curled up his neck from his left shoulder, its tongue lapping at his ear. Rebecca's name embraced his right bicep. USA circled his left. His chest bore a wild pastiche of Monet's *Water Liiles* and his calves the lightning bolts he had imagined. His back remained untouched because, he would explain, he could not see it without struggling with double mirrors. In fact, there were moments when looking in a mirror he didn't recognize himself. After so many years in one suit of skin, it took a few moments to adjust to the startling alternative.

***

Bob came home one night around 10 p.m. after a few drinks with Avery. The topic of their conversations since that seminal evening had changed from all about Avery to all about Bob. This night Bob had told his recent fishing stories with the passionate exaggerations of a true angler. Avery might not have agreed with the nature of Bob's transformation, but he knew he was the one who had saved Bob from his existential malaise. And Bob enjoyed blaming Avery for each new tattoo.

Opening the back door to the kitchen, Bob did not find Rebecca at the dinner table where she would normally wait for his return home from the restaurant. He called out to her. "Upstairs," she yelled down to him in an anxious tone. "Please, come up stairs now!"

He found her in the chair in the corner of the bedroom, her knees pulled up to her chest, one arm wrapped around them, the other behind them. "What is it?" he asked walking to her, noticing the tear stains on her cheeks and a convulsive trembling. "What's the matter?" he asked again kneeling down in front of her.

"There was someone in the house, walking through the house. I could hear him down there, in the kitchen. Then in the living room."

"When, Becca, when did you hear him?"

"About an hour ago. I think I heard him leave through the kitchen door. I was up here, thank God. I hid over there, behind the bed, under the bed. I would have called you but

22

was afraid they might hear me and find me." She pointed in the direction of the bed with a nod of her head, her arms still holding tight around her knees.

"Are you sure you heard him leave?"

"Pretty sure now, now that you're home." She paused for a moment. I've got the gun."

"You've got the gun?" He was surprised. "Where?" He didn't see it.

"Here." With the hand between her knees and chest, she pushed the gun out at him, her hand shaking, her finger on the trigger

"Becca! Don't point that at me. Here, let me have it." He put his hand out to take the gun. She pulled it back.

"Were you here earlier? Before you came home?"

"What are you saying? Of course not. That doesn't make any sense. "

"Yes, it does. Tell me you were here earlier in the kitchen looking for something." The anxiety in her voice was escalating.

"I'll tell you what. I will go down stairs and check things out, secure the house. We need to be sure whoever it was is gone. OK? But I'll need the gun just in case, OK?"

"No! It's my gun. I won't feel safe without it."

Bob got up off his knees and looked down at his wife. He had never seen her look so vulnerable.

"We should have gotten two," she said.

"Two what?"

"Two guns."

"Becca, this is not the time for this, for analyzing past decisions. If you won't give it to me, I'll go without it." Bob walked toward the stairs, believing she would reconsider, but found himself heading down to the kitchen without the gun. He didn't believe there was anyone in the house. He had locked all the doors when he had left to meet Avery, and the kitchen door was locked when he came home. The intruder would not have been able to lock the kitchen door behind him. Whatever Rebecca had heard, it wasn't an intruder—maybe a squirrel in the attic or something moving in a wall. Even so, he was purposefully cautious, going from room to room and into the basement, all lights on, all corners explored, all doors and windows closed and locked.

"All clear," he announced entering the bedroom, looking toward the empty chair where he had left her. He saw the light on in the bathroom and walking toward it, repeated the phrase. She poked her head out the door. "Thanks, honey. Thanks for being so brave." It sounded almost as if she was making fun of him and it rankled him.

"You're welcome. What are you doing?"

"Just getting ready for bed, now that I feel safe."

"Where's the gun?"

"I have it with me of course."

Bob sat down in the chair where she had been sitting and waited for her. She seemed to take forever. The adrenaline surge had faded and he was exhausted. What was taking so long? Was she hiding in there now, sitting on the edge of the tub with the gun pointed at the door? He needed to pee and went down to the kitchen bathroom.

She was in bed when he returned. On her side, facing the wall, knees drawn up to her chest. He was confused by her seeming composure after so much angst and the insincere tone of her expressed gratitude. That conversation, so many years ago, about getting a gun came back to life. It distracted him while putting his pajamas on and as he walked into the bathroom. He was remembering his earlier concerns when he saw the gun sitting on top of the toilet tank.

Why would she leave it behind, leave it there of all places? A surge of anxiety tightened his neck. He picked it up, so it rested on his palm, the trigger lying near his index finger. He stared at the gun, then straightened his arm and raised it level with his face, his eyes looking down the barrel and remembered the day they bought it. How the box it sat in rested on her lap as he drove. He felt again the strange fear that had entered his comfortable world that day. He would return the gun to its box under the bed. They would need to talk about this in the morning.

He turned toward the bathroom door to leave, suddenly surprised to see a man he did not recognize reflected in the mirror above the sink, facing him, gun in hand, pointed at him. Confused and without thinking Bob pulled the trigger, the mirror shattering, the bullet piercing the wall behind it, lodging in the back of the headboard of the bed where Rebecca slept.

Magneto

Pity the poor male mosquito
Who lives just ten days, incognito.
He'd never confess
His life is a jest;
It would just damage his ego.

A few days to find the right female,
Fall in love, then die the next day.
It just wasn't right
To give up one's life,
Not knowing the spawn he had made.

A mosquito named Magneto
Espoused an outrageous credo:
His life to exist
Beyond coital bliss
His children to finally behold.

It was such a huge leap of faith
To think he could alter his fate,
Defying the gods
Against all the odds
So his ambition he could sate.

His buzz was much louder than most.
His wingspan a size he could boast.
To build up his strength
He pressed from a bench
The heaviest thing he could hold.

On day three of his fragile life
He met his most beautiful wife.
Not knowing his fate,
She agreed to taste
The sweet nectar of paradise.

Next day he was proud as could be
And in search of his progeny.
He flew to a bog
And there by a log
A small worm was all he could see.

He expected to meet his child,
But larvae were all he could spy.
Small tears filled his eyes.
Clouds darkened the sky
As his will to live expired.

God and Celestial Light

God was in the laboratory when Celestial Light arrived. It was not unusual to find Light in the lab, watching God work, creating all kinds of things. She was there that momentous day when God set off the big bang. Such a huge step. The laboratory shook, startling them both. With the concussion, Celestial fragmented momentarily into radiant particles, and every shade of every color flickered through infinite space.

Celestial, reconstituted, was beautiful. A paradigm of color, her shape a wavering hexagon of shifting hues. She recognized her indebtedness to God in the beauty of her construction, as she was not created in God's image. God was merely an incandescence, a ghost light of changing form.

Today she had a concern to raise with God about a new experiment. The two were on good terms. She was an acolyte who always showed her deference, and this would be the first time she would offer a suggestion of her own. She had watched God choose one planet in particular for this most recent effort, not that there was much "effort" involved. It was a small planet in a small galaxy. God had always started small, at least until the big bang. The experiment was to create various forms of mortal life on the orb. Mortality was a new concept, since both God and Celestial Light were timeless. The idea came to God after the big bang. What had been a vast emptiness was no longer, and a universe of possibilities was the new reality.

God was energized by the project, busy creating mortal

life forms. The idea of one would evolve into an idea of another. But it was taking more time than God had hoped. Time was the new concept that drove the experiment, since mortality cannot exist without time. God found the idea both a gift and a nuisance. The anxiety and frustration that accompanied time were unanticipated and unwelcome by-products, even though God had created them both and could at any moment destroy them.

Mortality raised the question of sustainability. The thought of these creations having a timespan, only to disappear forever, was an anathema for God. After much thought the idea of reproduction emerged. What if they disappeared but came to life again, the same but different, each a new creation, created by the original creation. There had to be a mechanism for that independent of God's will. It was from this dilemma that the concepts of seed and gender were born. God revelled in the infinite variations these themes allowed.

Celestial Light loved the idea of reproduction and chose for herself the gender that birthed new life and nurtured it into its glorious final form.

It was in this context that Celestial Light raised a question. "You've been doing some wonderful things in the lab lately," she said. "That planet you're working on is so colorful and vibrant, the landscape so varied and alive. You've even given names to your creations, something you haven't done before. You explained to me how they interact with each other, the seas and the land, the plants and the animals, the rain and the clouds and the flowers and the bees. I could go on and on. It is incredible how it all fits together."

God's incandescence flickered. "This has been a work of wonder for me," God said quietly, "wondering what to create next and how it will connect to what has come before, how each creation enables the next. I can see no end to this, at least for now." Now was also a new concept, given the creation of time.

Light returned to her objective. "I have a question for you, if you don't mind."

"Of course," God replied.

"You have created creation itself. Your oak trees grow those small seeds that drop to the ground to create more trees. Fruit trees flower to attract the bees to make the seeds so each fruit tree can create more trees. And many of your creatures have been made in two forms, one to create the seeds and one to accept and grow them, each with the instinct to do what it must do. As you know, I have chosen the latter. Your mind is so wonderfully rich with alternatives to allow mortal life to perpetuate itself forever."

"Yes," God responded. "That's the idea- immortality through mortality"

"But shouldn't each of those creatures be able to appreciate what you have designed?"

"What do you mean?" God asked.

"Let me give you an example. Think about the eels you made, the ones with the long fins. Not one of your more attractive creatures, I must say, but not as ugly as the hagfish. I don't really know what you were thinking with that project. But back to the eels, you have them live a very, very long life. One of the longest lives of all the creatures on the planet, so far."

"Yes, I know," God replied. "That was my experiment with longevity. I don't know the word 'ugly'. Did you just make that up?"

"It's not the horrible face I am concerned about," Light continued. "It's the design of their reproduction. It's in the last year of their long life that they want to mate. And then you've made some special place, far, far away from their home, where they must swim to find a mate and plant the seed and then," she paused for effect, "they immediately die. Just like that. They never see their offspring. Never get the chance to appreciate your wondrous life-giving gift."

"Yes," God said. "I didn't think I had to worry about that."

31

That God could worry was inconceivable to Light, but then God embodied all things. "I don't mean to be critical," Light continued. "I think what you're doing is beyond belief. But there's something missing that I didn't understand until I thought more about the eel. Something I didn't even recognize in myself until now. I feel badly for them and for you. I want your creations to know that they have created life. I want them to appreciate your gift of immortality through their children. How do they even know what they have accomplished if they die before they see their offspring? I have discovered that I have feelings, feelings for these ugly eels. They must have feelings too. Do they?"

"Feelings? Well, no," God responded. "They don't even think. That's what instinct is for, so they will do what they need to do without thinking. If these creations had feelings, were thoughtful, they couldn't survive. They'd make bad choices. They wouldn't kill for their food, for example, feeling sorry about the killing. They would know fear and hesitate and become vulnerable to all kinds of danger."

"Are you sure?" Light asked.

"I'm sure."

"So, they are better off?"

"Yes. I don't care if they appreciate what I have done or not. They're definitely better off if they can't appreciate or feel."

"So, I would be wasting my time if I also mentioned a similar situation for the mosquito?"

"Yes," God said, "but I'll tell you what. I'm about to create the most complex of all creatures. I'm using the chimps that swing in the forest trees as my template. This new one will walk upright on two legs, have a larger brain. I'll make it to think beyond instinct. If you want, I will add feelings. We can find out together how much they will appreciate each other and my work."

Celestial Light couldn't believe what she heard. "Oh yes," she said. "Thank you, God. I love that you have listened to

me and considered my opinions worthy."
God's incandescence flickered in reply.

Magritte

There once was a piggy from Scranton
Who vowed she'd never be fattened.
After seeing the fate
Of her much larger mates,
She hitchhiked her way to Manhattan.

She painted her hoof with a thumb
That sparkled like gems in the sun,
Caught the eye of a boar
Who thought her a whore,
And offered a ride for some fun.

She did not understand his intentions
'Til he turned in the wrong direction.
With his hand on her knee,
Saying "I like 'em lean.
Carrying any infections?"

Her mind was confused and unfocused;
Did he think she had trichinosis?
With her head in a spin,
The truth ushered in
And she leapt from the car while in motion.

Her name was Magritte, by the way,
No ordinary pig, they would say.
With the farmer's shout
"Eat your slop or get out,"
She would roll in the mud and play.

As she stood by the side of the road
Not knowing which way to go,
She prayed to Demeter
Good fortune would greet her
And stuck out her thumb to the flow.

Magritte

She knew she had lost consciousness when she found herself waking up on the side of the road. Her first thought was to stand up, but neither her will nor energy could conjure that feat. A line of asphalt like a crust of charred bacon wriggled down her flank. A blunt pain throbbed above her left ear as blood oozed from the edges of road stones embedded in her knees.

It was not what she had wanted to do, jump out at 60 miles an hour. It was more like a falling out, actually, pressing her weight through her shoulder against the door, closing her eyes, yanking the handle, letting velocity and gravity spill her to the road like trash off the back of a pickup.

He had seemed safe enough at first. His hooves appropriately spaced at 10 and 2 on the wheel, he kept his eyes on the road, except when they ticked up to the rearview mirror appearing to concentrate on the traffic.

She followed his gaze, looking straight head, ignoring the vistas on either side, the tumble of hills with silos like beacons shining above the trees. She missed the farm, the cool of the barn floor, the dim light, the air a mangled breath of hay and manure.

His sparse black beard poked from his face, so many skinny wires with no purpose. A dark leathery snout twitched with each intake of air. "Where you headed?" he had asked.

"Manhattan," she said

"What's in Manhattan?" he wondered.

"I don't know," she answered.

"You got family there? In the city?"

She had left her family at the farm, six brothers and sisters, born minutes apart, squealing and pushing each other at the trough in a crush of appetite, getting bigger by the day. *I won't have a family much longer*, she had thought.

Given the monotony of the ride, her thoughts wandered from the road to the farm, then back. She knew why she had left her family, but she did not know where she was going. "Manhattan" was just a word she had heard in the stall as the farmer's wife forked fresh hay to its floor while talking to her sister. "Got to get back to Manhattan," the sister had said. It was a curiosity Magritte could not get out of her head. She liked the sound of it, the way each syllable rhymed. It became like a mysterious song.

***

After some time had passed, she asked "Is this the way to Manhattan? Are we going the right way?"

"What did I say when you got in? I'll take you as far as the Emerald Lakes. Then you can catch a ride on 80. You don't trust me? Why'd you get in? A pretty thing like you with a hoof out on a major highway is a sight to behold." He took his eyes off the road to catch her reaction, snorted and winked. "There's a rest stop up ahead I gotta use. We'll be turnin' off in a minute or two."

***

It was a simple question, she thought, one of those questions we often ask ourselves, like "Am I doing this right? Why am I doing it at all?" Existential questions. *I thought I saw a sign pointing ahead to Wilkes-Barre*, she said to herself. The signs to Manhattan had all pointed in the opposite direction.

***

The rest stop was a quaint log cabin, replete with vending machines, an information kiosk and a large highway map in a wood frame by the entrance. Instead of going inside, the boar trotted into the brush beside the cabin.

Magritte walked to the map hoping to get a sense of where she was. She didn't know what to make of its yellow and green lines going every which way and blobs of blue shaped like shovels with white numbers. He had said the number 80 and after a search she found it on a green line. She traced it with her dew claw, back and forth from one side of the map to the other, but she didn't know where she was and couldn't get her bearings. Maybe running from the farm was a mistake, she thought. Maybe she wasn't meant to do this, to determine her own fate. She looked to the woods on either side of the cabin wanting a path, a woods road instead of a highway to take her back to the farm.

He was suddenly beside her. "Here you are," he said. "What are you doing? Can you tell where we are from that map?"

"No," she admitted.

He pointed to an arrow poised at a black dot. "Here," he said, "we're here. Now let's get back in the car." Turning to the parking lot he looked over his shoulder at her. What choice did she have except to follow?

***

As the car pulled out onto the highway, she winced as the sun caught the top of the windshield, blinding her. It was late afternoon, she guessed, and thought it odd they were facing the sun. Afternoon at the farm the sun would pour into the pen behind the barn, casting a soothing amber light by sunset. Her thoughts went back to the map—Manhattan on one side, Wilkes-Barre on the other. She might not know the map terminology, but she knew the limited universe of her life—the mysterious woods road beyond the pen, how morning light filled the huge door at the barn's other end. She remembered the afternoon they all had escaped the pen, rooted the lawn at the front of the house, and ambled to freedom down the dirt road from the house until the farmer coaxed them back with the slop bucket. It was the only true moment of freedom she had known until this day, expanding her map of the world exponentially.

Riding with the boar, she suddenly became even more convinced she was heading the wrong way in a car racing somewhere she didn't want to go. He took his hand off the wheel, leaned toward her, his dew claw suddenly sliding down her leg. "I like 'em lean" he said.

It was then that instinct prevailed. She pushed her shoulder into the door, shut her eyes, and yanked the door handle. As she fell from the car her rear hooves flailed up, kicking him in the face. She tumbled across the road's shoulder, and rolled into the weeds. Knocked unconscious by the fall, she didn't see the car weaving down the highway, out of control, flipping over the guardrail into a river below.

The Martian

There once was a creature on Mars
Who drove Lamborghini cars,
Drank scotch at the bars,
Smoked Cuban cigars,
A confidant to movie stars

Who sent it their fears and questions,
About their fellow civilians,
Who gawked at their homes,
Invaded their phones,
And proclaimed ardent affection.

The Martian had no known gender,
But that didn't bother these senders
Of queries and thoughts
Re: fans and consorts
And whether to wear silk or leather.

The Martian rode a satellite
Around the earth, both day and night,
Exchanging wisdom
About the prison
The movie stars said was "the life"

That all the earthlings aspired to.
And what were those stars to do?
Imprisoned by fame,
Good fortune to blame
For this their unfortunate due?

The Martian knew nothing of fame,
Notoriety, or acclaim.
In actual stars,
The planets afar,
All beings are treated the same.

It's advice was as ignorant
As a new-born wide-eyed infant's.
The stars didn't care
The Martian had flaire—
The cigars, car, and an accent.

Angry Archie Thrasher

Angry Archie Thrasher was not easy to like because he always presented as hostile and aggravated. It was the dark, sharp tone of his voice, the abrupt movements of his hands that sliced the air for emphasis, the rapid speech, the way he'd cross his arms and stare into your eyes. It could be the most mundane subject in the most comfortable of settings where anger should have no residence when he seemed the most irritable. When asked to describe him, acquaintances and colleagues used terms like "contentious" or "crotchety" or "unapproachable." Thus, he came to be known as Angry Archie.

It was his real self. But Archie was an actor by vocation and with the cameras rolling was able to act like a thoughtful, mild-mannered individual. It was in these parts that he was surprisingly most effective. On *Law and Order* he was cast as the sensitive, anguished cop, facing interrogation, falsely accused of tampering with a crime scene. In a *Lifetime* movie he was the family man who cried when accused of killing his neighbor's dog. He could be cast as a short-term love interest, the sympathetic relative at a funeral, a bumbling co-worker, or a thoughtful counselor. But off camera he was always himself.

His agent hated working for him. His wife had left him. His old friends avoided him. He never admitted that his nervous system had been affected by his stint as a paratrooper at the Battle of Junction City in Vietnam, dropping into blade-whipped roiling meadows ringed by trees hiding the Vietcong.

A little over five feet tall, thin as a two-packs-a-day smoker, his face prematurely crevassed from the habit, he looked like a crusty, aging criminal.

It was by chance that he discovered the Martian. Surfing the web for films in their pupa stage with roles that might find life through his strengths, a pop-up invaded the screen: "CAN I BE OF HELP?" Curious, and against his better judgement, Archie clicked on it.

"Help with what?" he asked."WHATEVER A MOVIE STAR NEEDS HELP WITH" was the response. He knew the internet was spying on everyone and his ever-present anger elevated. Archie clicked out of the dialogue box, only to see the pop-up return. He shut down his computer, grabbed a cigarette and went for a walk.

His acting parts, though small, had paid him relatively well and, with few expenses, he had treated himself to a modest bungalow overlooking L.A. Living alone with time to kill between jobs, he could often be found walking the streets of his upscale neighborhood for hours, hoping to hike out the demons that possessed him. He knew he spent too much time in his own head. The therapy that failed him after the war had at the very least taught him that. So had the drugs he had turned to after the alcohol had lost its power over his PTSD. Each supposed cure was like reliving the parachute jumps during the war - the rush of anticipation, the thrill of the leap into space and free fall, the jolt of the opening chute slowing his descent as fear of his approaching death raced through his nerves, almost disabling him. It was also analogous to his marriage and relationships with former friends.

On this walk Archie could not leave the internet message behind. He was angry and felt violated. Who was this asking to help? What kind of help? For what? Why him? What did this person know about him? About his career? He was certain it was some kind of scam to get inside his financials. Was there a way to find out without exposing himself even more? Or should he just ignore it? Why bother with it? It will just go away, he predicted, but, then again, maybe it wouldn't. If he had to, as much as he hated to, he'd change his internet identity.

After considerable debate with himself, he did just that. The next day he bought a new computer, set up a new email address and web server under a different password, and sent postcards off to those who'd need to know. Not confident that he had completely protected himself, he reluctantly avoided his technology for a week, suffering through what he believed to be a cleansing abstinence.

It was on a starlit Saturday night a week later that he hesitantly returned to cyberspace, only to have the pop-up return, this time addressing him by name.

"ARCHIE, HOW CAN I BE OF HELP? CAN WE TALK? CLICK ON THE ICON OF THE MICROPHONE IN THIS MESSAGE."

Feeling defeated and angry with himself for not seeking assistance at the Genius Bar, he slammed his fist on the table, stood up, and paced the room, shouting "Stupid fool!" and "Damned idiot!" at himself. His hands shaking, grabbing his cigarettes, he walked out the door. "Why am I so stupid?" he asked himself. "What do I know about technology?"

A breeze cooled by the Pacific brushed across his face. The lights of L.A. exposed a few ragged clouds below bright shimmering stars as Archie stopped at the end of his driveway to collect himself. He was looking to the night sky for succor. *There's little difference between outer space and cyberspace,* he thought. *Both are mysterious and unfathomable. Don't we take a leap of faith every time we board a plane? Or enter the internet? Do we ever really know what's out there? How was whatever fell out of the sky at Roswell any different from this mysterious visitor on his browser? What was he afraid of? Somebody out there thought he needed help. He knew he did.*

Archie Thrasher walked back up his driveway, stopping once again to scan the iridescent sky. Once in the house he opened his Mac. He had left it on. The question starred back at him. He hit the microphone icon and uttered an uncharacteristically tentative "Hello."

The response was an immediate and robust "Mr. Thrasher?" in an accent he did not recognize.

"Who are you?" Archie asked.

"I am a counselor to the stars, Mr. Thrasher. I have references if you'd care to see them."

"I didn't ask you what you are. I asked you who you are," Archie responded in his typical angry tone. "What is your name? Where are you? Somewhere in L.A. or New York, I presume.

"Not even close. Tell me, Mr. Thrasher, how can I help you? I have helped so many of your colleagues - Robert Wagner, Demi Moore, Johnny Depp, Angie Dickinson, Lon Chaney. Oh, and come to think of it, Boris Karloff's wives. I have references."

"You still haven't answered my questions," Archie responded. "And these people are not my colleagues. I am lucky if I get a small part in one of their movies. I'm a character actor. What is your name? Where are you? Why are you on my computer?"

"Are your fans bothering you, Mr. Thrasher? That is my specialty, you know, creating a mental and emotional space for thespians between themselves and their fawning fans. I helped Lon maintain a very private life. Boris, on the other hand, was a serial philanderer. I counseled his ex-wives. I tried to help Johnny, but quite frankly, he is his own worst enemy. I am out here literally circling the planet to help stars in need. I am here to help you."

This was going nowhere for Archie who had little tolerance for indifference to his needs. It was like those unwanted robocalls that so infuriated him. But he did not want to let go. Someone wanted to help him, a fact which had not been the case for a long time. He knew he needed help. His loneliness was only mitigated by his work and that was sporadic.

Here he was desperately needing a conversation with this someone who wouldn't even answer a couple simple questions.

Archie's frustration with the tack of the conversation suddenly suggested a different approach. "Okay, whoever you are," he answered, "what do you charge?"

"I do not charge," the martian answered, "but I do accept gifts."

"What kind of gifts?"

"Boris's wife Evelyn bequeathed a Lamborghini to me when she died. I'm sitting in it right now. I've had it modified. Christian Bale keeps me well stocked with 21-year-old Glenlivet, though I don't think I deserve it, since I have not seen much change in his ability to deal with his fans, admiring or otherwise."

"You know, I don't really have admiring fans or fans at all," Archie confessed. "I don't even think my agent is a fan. Are you an agent? Can you find me work?"

"No, but I can help you over the rough spots, the dry spells. I can give your life a whole other dimension, take you to a better space, lift you out of this world you have made for yourself. I think you're ready. I've been watching you the whole of your professional life. Well, maybe not the whole of it. But ever since your outburst on the set of that *Blue Steel* movie when you angrily threw the wine bottle at Jamie Lee Curtis. It was a good thing she saw it coming. You could have killed her. Instead, you pretty much killed your career for the rest of that year. I'm here for you, Mr. Thrasher. Take another walk and clear your head if you need to. Let's talk again tomorrow night, same time. Agreed?"

Archie, incredulous and speechless, nodded his head.

"Good. Okay then. It's a deal. See you then."

Suddenly Archie realized that he had not uttered a word of assent about another conversation. "Wait a minute. Give me a second," Archie pleaded. "How did you know I agreed about tomorrow night? Can you see me somehow? How do you know about the walks?" But the dialogue box had disappeared. He desperately searched the screen, looking for it among the folders on his desktop. It was gone.

Closing his computer, Archie suddenly realized the guy could see him with or without the computer. How else would he know his private moments? How on earth did he know about those? How was that even possible? His heart spiked, and a ragged current rippled up his back with the recognition of his utter desperation for a relationship, any relationship.

Tomorrow night; he couldn't wait. Tomorrow night. He needed answers. He needed to talk.

Tommy

Tommy was thought a wunderkind.
A prodigy, a special kid.
When very young
He spoke in tongues,
To some a blessing, some a sin.

Or was it just childish babble
From a hyper boy who'd prattle
On and on
From dawn to dawn
Indecipherable matters.

Some claimed he knew what others didn't,
That he was prescient or omniscient.
A towhead boy
In Illinois,
A petri dish of contradictions.

He should have been more self-aware,
Given his persona's glare
Set him apart
From peers and hearts
And minds of those within his sphere.

His grasp of life seemed sporadic,
His common sense quite erratic—
A cross to bear
He couldn't share.
To most he was just problematic.

What happens to that different child
When he leaves his youth behind -
His universe
Voluminous,
His future path so hard to find?

Fall back on what he's come to know?
Be himself, accept the blows
That fall on those
Whose actions sow
That well-known fear of the unknown?

Ipse Dixit

Young Tommy Jaworski's head was full of words. He couldn't get away from them. Real words and words he made up by assembling sounds that resembled them. Sounds that rhymed or repeated consonants like a stutter. Or hummed like a melody. While playing with his toys he would talk to himself this way, his voice rising and falling, starting and stopping, mimicking a conversation without recognizable words. He was an only child and his parents thought his utterances and odd conversations were just part of a typical child's development. His behavior indicated that he understood their words and wishes, like "no," and "bedtime" and "let's play." At times he would mimic them and act as if to affirm their intent, but on most occasions his responses were unrecognizable.

Once in school Tommy was in an environment where his eccentric behavior was glaringly notable. While he responded to teacher requests behaviorally, he often appeared unable to answer questions or engage in conversations with a coherent string of words. Special education services were called in to identify his disability but were unable to diagnose a particular syndrome or handicapping condition. His parents remained sanguine in the face of expressed concerns regarding their son, noting his mild demeanor, extreme concentration and improbable ability to solve kinetic challenges. Put a hands-on problem before him and he would meet it with focus and speed, all the while talking to himself in a language his peers called "Tommy talk."

Tommy presented an intensity of appearance. Curly blond hair sat above a face of dark complexion. His large brown eyes rarely blinked and appeared to constantly stare at the focus of his attention. The movements of his head were often abrupt as that focus snapped from one target of consideration to another. And, of course, there was his talking to himself in rapid sentences with unintelligible words in an erratic cadence that seemed to rise and fall like fleeting expressions of anxious emotion.

School specialists finally decided that he presented as autistic and would remain in the regular classroom with support as needed. Over time, his behavior became less abnormal, more a novelty and distraction. He excelled in music class and hands-on science. A voracious reader, he would finish two books to his classmates' one and answer the worksheet questions accurately with many obscure but real words. His teachers avoided asking him questions during class discussions, but if he volunteered, his answers were deconstructed and politely accepted. Students learned to ignore his hyperactivity and rarely interacted with him. Except for Olivia Henderson, the classmate with the pig tails and freckles and bright eyes.

By chance, Olivia was the fourth-grade student assigned the desk closest to him at the back of the room. She was at first unhappy with the assigned seat but did not complain. As the year progressed, however, her initial stoicism turned to sympathy for Tommy's self-inflicted ostracism. During the occasional lulls in class activities she would turn to him for conversation. Tommy seemed loath to respond at first, but gradually allowed himself to focus, if only briefly, on her approaches. His responses both surprised and delighted her. To her "How are you?" he would respond with *theosophic* or *mephitic*. She'd ask him to repeat himself and then spell the words. Finding their definition in her desk dictionary, she had to smile. The words were often oddly appropriate, which made her laugh, and had the effect of sparking her imagination. She gradually came to appreciate his eccentricity as a gift, bringing a fun distraction into bland school days.

Gradually the two grew closer. Toward the end of that school year they were eating lunch together and walking the perimeter of the playground in conversation during recess. She would ask him to use words she knew and Tommy would comply as best he could. She learned he was an only child, that his parents distanced themselves from him and generally left him alone, and that he had no neighborhood friends. While she struggled to follow his train of thought as his mind leapt from one topic to another, there was an exciting quality about each conversation, an energy field that radiated surprise.

Olivia recognized endearing and admirable features to Tommy's struggle to fill his loneliness with his preoccupation and love for language, its infinite variety and sound, and his compulsion to deconstruct anything that posed a problem into its ordered parts to relieve the anxiety it fostered. For nine-year-old Olivia each of these aspects of Tommy's reality was both magical and a cry for help.

Their friendship grew through middle school. Olivia would help him in social encounters with other students, leading those conversations forward as Tommy veered off topic, explaining Tommy's comments, and ignoring his drifts into the unrelated. She invited him to her home for dinner, surprising her parents with her poise and understanding of his idiosyncrasies and with his odd but engaging company. Olivia became his compass to navigate the normal world, to assimilate the day-to-day, until the day she died.

It was a winter afternoon in their high school freshman year when they were walking home from school together that a car skidded across a slippery street and over the curb, killing Olivia and throwing Tommy onto the icy sidewalk, knocking him into a coma he would not escape for two weeks. When he did, words flooded his head, their sounds and shapes, but without any sense of meaning. They clouded his memory and vision. He did not recognize his parents who sat at his bedside, or know where he was. Nor could he remember his name or recall anything about his life.

The words swept by in a cavernous mental space, alone and strung together, appearing and then disappearing, criss-crossing each other, some floating about reluctant to leave. With his eyes open he saw them everywhere, sitting on the chair by his bed, or on the side table, in the small plastic pill cup, waiting to be swallowed. They would land on his blanket and then lift off, only to drift back. There was no escape. Even with a distraction like the arrival of the doctor or nurse or his parents, they lingered above incomprehensible conver-sations, wanting to interrupt, impatient for the intruder to leave. Some of his favorite words, the ones he loved to say, like obsequious, pusillanimous, and subcutaneous, drifted in and out of view. The angry ones that frightened and dimin-ished him, those that he had often heard behind his back, hovered on the edges.

Then one day a strange foreboding wrapped around this plague of words. Some coupled together and abruptly disap-peared leaving a void. Fewer hung on the edges. Those that remained were different from the others, more sinister and threatening, alarm bells that throbbed like pain. He sensed impending danger and the need to escape. With his eyes closed he shook his head vigorously, whipping it back and forth until the words disappeared. Suddenly, fully conscious, he realized that the woman sitting in the corner of the room half asleep was his mother. He slowly understood the reality of his condition, lying in a hospital room, weak, unsubstan-tial and tremendously tired. And then he remembered Olivia Henderson walking beside him and the flying car.

***

It took almost a year for Tommy to fully recover from the brain damage he had suffered, and even then, he found himself forgetting even recent experiences and newly learned facts. He struggled at times to articulate comprehensible thoughts. Most of the large and odd vocabulary he had assembled and enjoyed had escaped and with it the joy and pride he'd had exploiting it. It had defined him. He was no longer himself.

But he remembered Olivia, her vision coming to life as he imagined her beside him, his imaginary companion, reassuring him that he would get better, distracting him, offering up her own odd vocabulary to stimulate his. He was living in his head, as he always had, but this time she was there too, as guide and helpmate, as real as anyone else and more significant. He spoke to her as if she were sitting across a table from him, laughing at her jokes, asking her questions, telling her stories. He'd call out for her to join him wherever he went. They were inseparable.

Tommy met bi-weekly with his therapist, Dr. Corbet. Olivia joined them. At first the doctor would ask Tommy that she not attend, but he relented as Tommy shut down in her absence. Dr. Corbet soon understood that she was like his alter ego, a bridge to his old self. The doctor decided to treat her as present. He asked Tommy what Olivia thought and found the response much like what he expected from him. His ultimate goal was to have Tommy absorb her identity into his own so he could become whole again, and suggested that Tommy was as capable as she to address his symptoms. But that did not happen. Olivia's role in Tommy's consciousness exploded into such a formidable alliance that Tommy automatically deferred to her direction and opinions, rejecting any of the doctor's guidance that did not reflect hers. Tommy's responses to the doctor's professional suggestions were what Olivia thought, not Tommy, and any request for his own feelings on those matters only reiterated hers.

***

It was on a bright, blue-sky spring day at the end of that

year of therapy that Tommy took control of his life. At this appointment Dr. Corbet encouraged him to try to remember the words that he had loved, to reconstruct past utterances, to imagine their target and effect. The doctor used the word "solipsism," defining it for Tommy as the belief that we can only be certain of what exists in our minds, and suggested that Tommy's vocabulary, not Olivia's, projected his sense of self out into a questionable reality. Tommy immediately loved the word. "Solipsism." He repeated it over and over again until he identified with it. He played with its possible variations like *solipsistic* and *solipsistically*. The exercise drove Tommy back into his old world of words, awash with significance and pleasure. Tommy became again his obsessive-compulsive self, searching for and capturing those friendly, special words, the sound of which embodied their meaning or exploded his imagination into a logophile's rapture.

***

With the loss of Olivia and his distance from his parents, there was no counsel to guide Tommy into adulthood. He struggled through high school with little enthusiasm and no friends, immersing himself in books and word games, spending solitary afternoons and evenings with crossword puzzles, hangman, and sudoku. He thought little about a future self or purpose, and at 18 years old, with a life beyond his school days imminent, he was stranded in the present. Time had turned Tommy into a six-foot-tall young man with broad shoulders and a budding blonde beard, a sharp contrast to his diminutive parents. His stature and intense, focused expressions were eye-catching and imposing. In the spring of his senior year his parents suggested he find a job but were uncertain about what he was prepared for and if he could cope with an employer's expectations. His work in school had required diminishing supports over the years, but his teachers continued to pay close attention to his special needs into his senior year.

***

Leaving the school auditorium after his graduation ceremony, Tommy and his parents were unexpectedly greeted by
Olivia's. "Tommy Jaworski, is that you?"

Tommy abruptly turned to face the question, recognizing
the couple he had dined with numerous times years earlier.

"And your parents, you must be so proud," Jim
Henderson continued, extending a hand of greeting to them.
The two couples, both in their fifties, had met four years ago
at Olivia's funeral and at a subsequent visit with Tommy in
the hospital, but had not communicated in the intervening
three years. Tommy awkwardly stood by as they reintro-
duced themselves. A spontaneous vision of Olivia standing
beside the Hendersons appeared and Tommy was suddenly
awash with grief.

Jim Henderson approached Tommy. "I've been thinking
about you, young man, thinking about you a lot lately and
your friendship with Olivia. You were such true friends. I
know that our loss was yours as well. It must have been very
difficult for you. And here you are, of course, graduating as
she certainly would have, a future ahead of you. We'd love to
catch up, maybe have you and your parents over for dinner."
He looked to the Jaworski's, who were surprised by the invitation. "What do you think?" he asked them. "Dinner, next
weekend?"

***

The Henderson's lived three blocks away where the
homes scaled up, block by block. Tommy and his parents
walked the sidewalk to the Henderson's' home, a journey
that took them past the scene of the accident. They had not
considered this when leaving the house, and upon approach-

57

ing the spot, realizing the decision to walk was a mistake, they took tentative steps in a mournful silence, an unwelcome return to a painful time.

They were met at the Henderson's' door with a robust greeting, the Jaworski's reticence a stark contrast to their exuberant hosts. Ushered into the living room, offered drinks and hors d'oeuvres and shown their assigned seats on the plush blue sofa, discomfort straightened their backs and tightened their shoulders. Tommy remembered the house as a comforting space and the Henderson's as affable and sincerely interested in him. A slow-motion vision of a 14-year-old Olivia welcoming him into her home embraced him.

Settled in with his drink in the easy chair across from the Jaworski's, Jim Henderson held forth, an animated presence in a subdued room. "It seems odd that we never really met before the accident," he began "except for the calls, you know, inviting Tommy for dinner after he had walked Olivia home. We so enjoyed his company. Our conversations were quite interesting and unique, quite beyond his years. He had such a positive effect on Olivia, brought her out of her shell. I'd say he enriched her life."

This was a revelation for the Jaworski's' who had never understood their son's relationship with Olivia, never understood her interest in him, where others chose to ignore or distance themselves from him.

Jim Henderson looked to Tommy. "Like I mentioned at your graduation, I've been thinking a lot about you. Do you have plans for the summer?"

"Not exactly," Tommy responded. "I'm going to look for employment."

"He's not sure what he wants to do," Cyrus Jaworski interjected. "He's not going to college, so we're hoping he can find something with a future."

"No college, Tommy? Why's that? You're a smart kid," Jim Henderson asked, ignoring the boy's father.

Tommy's face flushed. Olivia's father should know why.

He'd experienced his disability first-hand. Tommy didn't want to have to remind him. "I'm on the autism spectrum," he explained, embarrassed, "obsessive-compulsive. My mind doesn't function like my peers, like yours. You know. I live in a world of words. I'm easily distracted. It's hard to explain."

"Yes, Olivia told us," Henderson replied. "Not with those words of course. I remember we so enjoyed our dinners with you, looked forward to them, those conservations at the table, animated by your vocabulary, your range of expression, the way one idea would ping off another. Right, honey?" Jim Henderson looked for affirmation from his wife and she smiled and nodded her agreement.

"It's why I've been thinking about you," Jim continued. "I've been sort of obsessed myself lately. Our law firm is looking for an intern. It's a paid position that could evolve into something permanent, like a legal aide. Typically, we'd be looking for a recent college graduate or one on summer break. But I thought of you. You'd be learning on the job. I know you'd find it interesting. The law is about stories; each case is a story. We build stories with the facts that we assemble. Every tort case is a mystery with a different twist. No two are alike. I remember those conversations at dinner about the books you were reading, how you could relate the stories with such detail. And how quickly you understood."

"And you would learn a new vocabulary," Rose interjected. "Words that would appeal to you, I think. English words and Latin ones like "ipso facto" and "ipse dixit." It's right up your alley."

Tommy laughed nervously, repeating the words aloud, turning to his parents who were speechless.

Then Cyrus Jaworski found his voice. "Are you sure this is a good idea?" he asked. "How well do you really know Tommy? He had a really rough go of it after the accident, for over a year, therapy and all that. It's only been in the last couple that he's seemed like his old self. We are thinking of something more physically active, more manual than mental, more solitary than social. He's a strong boy, landscaping, maybe."

Jim Henderson fell silent, unable to understand how his offer could be so summarily rejected. Did they not see the potential that he saw? Of course, they knew their son better than he did, but their direction for his future seemed such a mistake. He decided to change his tack.

Jim Henderson rose slowly from his easy chair. A tall man with considerable experience arguing cases before a jury, he towered above the Jaworski's on the blue sofa as he moved to stand beside his seated wife. "We've also been thinking a lot about Olivia lately," he continued, resting his hand on his wife's shoulder. "At first we weren't going to go to the graduation ceremony. We thought it would be too difficult for us, but we had lost track of her old school friends and wanted to see them again, you know, how they've changed over the last three years, and their future plans. Especially Rita Johnson and Beth Schulz. They'd been to the house many times for sleepovers and such."

"We were reminiscing recently about how Olivia's relationship with Tommy was so special. How well she understood him, appreciated and supported him. We could tell the feeling was mutual. There was a symbiosis, a simpatico between the two. Tommy brought out the best in her. The way she embraced and accepted him for who he was had quite an effect on us. It seemed almost instinctive for her.

"And there was a reciprocal quality to the relationship. Not like the golden rule that says do unto others as we would have them do unto us, like a dictate. It was more something innate, a natural force within the two of them, in their hearts, a kindness and generosity and support for each other."

Rose Henderson interrupted. "We saw ourselves deficient in that respect," she said looking up to her husband, then to the Jaworski's. "Not that we hadn't been generous with donations to this or that good cause. Not that we weren't sympa-

60

thetic to those in need. We were just sort of passive about it, kept a distance, where for Olivia and Tommy there was an intimacy and sincerity."

"Wait a minute!" Cyrus Jaworski came to life, his voice sharp. "What are you saying? Tommy's some kind of welfare case? And you're some kind of saints? Alms to the poor and all that? Our boy is eighteen. He's a man now. He's gotta make his own way in life. He knows his strengths and weaknesses. He just told you!" Jaworski grabbed his wife's arm, lifting her off the sofa as he stood. "Thanks for the drinks. You don't need to show us to the door. Come on, Tommy, we're leaving now."

Tommy barely heard the command. He had tuned out the conversation, imagining himself working in a law office, like he'd seen on TV, remembering the stories, the puzzles that had to be solved, the search for truth, and the way language had such power in the interrogations in the court room. He pictured himself arguing a case, using his words to full effect.

"Get up Tommy. Let's go! We're going home," he heard repeated, his father's strident voice slicing through his reverie and a vision of himself he would never have thought to imagine.

Premonition

Please consider the psychic dog -
Its sixth sense when something goes wrong -
The ears that perk up,
The growl that erupts,
The hair on its back standing tall.

Or imagine the psychic cat
Sound asleep on its owner's lap
Awake with a start
With fear in its heart
From dreams of a coming attack.

The buffalos of Bang Koey
Stopped grazing and looked toward the sea,
Then raced up a hill
To avoid being killed
Hours before a tsunami.

The villagers watched the stampede
Alarmed by the trumpeting beasts
Ran up behind them
Chasing the mayhem,
Escaping the violent sea.

In 373 B C
Historian Thucydides
Said that rats and snakes
Fled from a quake
Well before it felled Heliki.

So, what's to be made of all this?
Is premonition hit-or-miss?
Must humans rely
On animal signs
To learn if they are at risk?

Our premonitions ignored,
Cast aside, not being the norm,
Appear in a dream
Or a thought surreal,
Unacceptable, uninformed.

Ask the people of Aberfan
Who did not want to understand
The fraught foreboding
From dreams exposing
A tragedy so near at hand

That thousands of tons of slurry
Would come down the hill and bury
Their children at school,
An event so cruel,
And out of the ordinary.

Vanishing Point

He sat at the back of the room on a tall stool, high enough to see his students' canvases over the backs of their heads. The heels of his work boots, splattered with multiple colors in oils and acrylics, were wedged into the stool's lowest rung to give him purchase to straighten his back and keep his head high. The apron he wore protecting his flannel shirt and jeans bore the streaks and spots of time-worn hues. His gaze appeared intense, fixed on the young artists' final touches, but, in fact, his attention wandered, desperate to be somewhere, anywhere else. Something was bothering him. He just couldn't put his finger on it.

His name was Richard Umbridge, and these were his four second-year artists. The assignment was entitled "Vanishing Point." He told them he wanted something different from the paintings they had studied on the subject—Caspar Friedrich's *The Cross in the Mountains* with the vertical lines of the church coming together at the cross in the sky, and Frits Thaulow's *The Train Is Arriving* with its obvious vanishing point at the end of railroad tracks converging on the train. The clearest example was Dali's *Agnostic Symbol*, the elongated spoon, its extenuated handle vanishing in an odd window in the top-right corner of the painting.

Richard wanted a more subtle manifestation, something that would unconsciously draw the eye into the distance. In each case the oculus would have to be different, the viewer's eyes focused from the left or right or even a bit above or below the painting, but not at the center. Wyeth's *Christina's*

World was an excellent example, he'd say, as he traced the viewer's attention from the woman, up the hill to the house and beyond.

Melissa had chosen to paint a mountain scene with a vanishing point above the mountaintop in the upper-left corner of her canvas. She had painted yellow grasses in the lower-right meadow bending toward the subtle mountain ridges that grew closer together, ascending up the mountainside to draw the eye to a point in the sky.

Andrea's painting was of an angry ocean at night, the sea foam sweeping left to right seeming more hostile as it lifted to the horizon toward the light of a clouded moon in the top-right corner.

A dark room with a window open to the morning light was Grace's effort, the slanted lines of the room's wood floor directing the viewer's eye up and out the window to the branch of an apple tree in blossom, barely visible, as if disappearing, in the top-right corner pane.

George had chosen an urban scene, a darkened city street. It was the space between the road's center line and its curb that grew narrower as it tilted up and left to meld with a woman at a bus stop, a street light illuminating her head and shoulders.

From what he could see, Richard was satisfied that three of his four students could technically apply the vanishing point concept, but he did not see in their efforts what he always hoped for, what he called "the wonderful." He wanted his students' art to ask the viewer to wonder why this subject, why these colors, why this technique and this effect. Richard believed that the best paintings raise questions without expecting answers, that they seek wonder for its own sake. Think Mona Lisa's smile, he would say, or Dali's *Persistence of Memory*, or Turner's *Great Western Railway*. Think of the questions they raise and how elusive the answers.

He wanted his students to apply a vanishing point that

would lead the viewer's thoughts away from a painting's obvious subject to a place of mystery and speculation. Richard slipped off his stool and walked to the front of his class. He lifted his baseball cap above his head, brushed his hair back, and stuck the cap into the back pocket of his jeans. Assuming a thoughtful posture, bending forward, he surveyed the paintings while pulling at his full beard. "George," he said, "bring your canvas up front please. Let's all take a look at your work."

Seeming reluctant at first, George complied, setting his painting on the chalk tray below the blackboard. He was 20 years old, a college sophomore with a 16-year-old's face. Richard stroked his beard and looked at the painting. "I'm not sure this is what I was looking for," he began. "My eyes follow the road and curb to the bus stop and the woman's feet and want to stay on the same trajectory, but get distracted by the cone of light over her head and, more importantly, by the street light pole that directs my eye up and away from the vanishing point, which I think should be in the shadows behind the base of the light pole. Am I right? Do you see what I mean?"

George reviewed his painting for a long moment. Without turning back to Richard, he quietly said, "yes."

"What do you think you should do about it?" Richard asked as he walked backward to stand among the other students.

"Well, I guess I should remove the street light," George said hesitantly.

"Anything else?"

"The woman?"

"What about her?"

"Remove her too?"

"What if you sat her down."

"On the curb?"

"Yes. Think about it. If she's standing, she's just waiting for a bus, but if she's sitting on the curb, it makes you wonder why. Could you change her posture, the angle of her shoulders, so as to continue the line of the road to take the viewer's eye beyond her, into the dark, beyond the canvas to whatever mysteries might lie there? That would be wonderful, don't you think? Two questions for the viewer, then: why is she sitting on the curb and what lies beyond her?"

George was speechless and looked to his classmates for help.

Richard suddenly realized he had piled on. George was struggling and clearly embarrassed. "I'm sorry, George, if I'm making my point at your expense," Richard said finally. "You can take your painting back to your easel."

Richard brushed his hair back, put his hat on and said, "I'll see you guys next time. Class dismissed. Let's tidy up."

***

Richard spent his drive home second-guessing himself. He knew he had embarrassed George. He could just as easily have spoken to him quietly at his easel, let him make changes to his painting before the end of class. But he didn't. It wasn't like him to use the power of his position this way. He had been on edge for days—quick to anger, restless, unable to concentrate. He was bored with his art, struggled with simple decisions, and sometimes became so distracted by random thoughts that he lost track of what he was about to do or where he was about to go. He diagnosed himself *depressed.*

He had been teaching for 13 years and a serious painter for 10. The teaching covered his expenses; his painting maintained his sanity. Like his students, he had dreamed of being a successful artist whose works received critical acclaim and a popularity that provided him a comfortable living. But in those 10 years he had sold only three paintings, and his studio served more as a storage closet than a work space. More importantly, his job was as adjunct faculty with no benefits or job security. The provost could decide at any time that he was no longer needed.

It was February, 6 p.m., 20 degrees, and the sun had set. Driving home, his head lights showed him only ten feet ahead at best. With no streetlights or porch lights or glow from windows, the trees at the edge of this country road were dark amorphous shadows. Lost in thought, he suddenly realized he didn't know where he was. There was little to see, and what he could see was unfamiliar. The few houses he had passed were unrecognizable. Did he miss the turn, the turn on to the dirt road that led to the collection of houses along the pond? The drive home had become automatic. He no longer had to pay much attention. Even so, he should know where he was.

Richard slowed to spend as much time looking toward the edge of the road as he did straight ahead. It didn't help. A car came up behind him hugging his trunk, headlights on full, shining off his rear-view mirror into his eyes. He pulled off to the side of the road to let it pass. *My God, what is going on?* he asked himself. *Maybe I should just turn around until I get to a place I recognize. Or maybe I can shake it off,* he thought. *A blast of cold will turn my head in the right direction.* Leaving his car running he got out, the headlights splashing the edges of the lower trunks of the tall oaks and poplars that rose skyward. Leaning against the right fender, he shivered as his eyes followed the tree trunks upward, his head canting back until he could see the night sky above their bare limbs, the white dots of stars like shimmering pebbles. He took a deep breath.

It was then that he had the premonition. He saw himself sitting in front of the provost's desk and the short, chubby man with the round face, the bald head, and the paisley bow tie who was leaning back in his chair. "We won't need you next term," he heard the provost saying. "We've looked at the numbers. You just don't have enough students to warrant the position. The number has been dropping each year. Four students in a class is too few. It doesn't pay us enough to pay you."

Richard rubbed his cold forehead. The irony of the vision was not lost on him, that the lesson these last few weeks was the vanishing point.

Expectations

Little Albert had never met
A rat he didn't want to pet
Or just ignore
'Less he was bored
'Til Watson manufactured dread.

Each time a rat came near the boy
Watson made a dreadful noise.
With vicious swings
His hammer pinged
A pipe so loud It scared the boy.

When Watson took the noise away,
Brought in the rat while Albert played,
Young Albert wailed,
Very afraid
Of the noise he'd anticipate.

The Little Albert Experiment
Was to prove this hypothesis:
A natural response
To a natural prompt
Can be changed to something different

When accompanied by stimuli
That completely override
The original,
Benign signal
To send us down a different slide.

Where Pavlov worked with animals
To prove conditioning's manacles,
John Watson chose
A 9-month-old
To prove his hypothetical.

Johnson

Johnson at age 75 claimed that he woke up every morning with a different ache or pain, the origin of which was often inexplicable, largely because most days in his 76th year of life were pretty much the same. His body would not sleep past 5:45 a.m. because it was the time he had alarmed himself awake for the 45 years of his working life. Now, in his empty retirement, with no alarm, he regained consciousness at 5:45 a.m. whether he wanted to or not.

At first, he tried to will himself back to sleep, but found that a futile effort. He experimented with counting back from a thousand, but would lose track of where he was in the count and give up. Then he started going to bed later and later each night, but surrendered after exposing himself to Kimmel, Colbert, and Fallon in rotation for a month only to wade through the fog of longer days.

Johnson wondered if the aches and pains were a consequence of his shrinking from six feet to five-ten, from a 34-inch waist to 31. He had taken to wearing suspenders to keep his pants up unable to justify buying new ones that he assumed would not fit for very long. Maybe the suspenders were the source of the recurring pain in his shoulders, he wondered. Maybe the lack of cinch around his waist aroused the old hernia pangs that had returned years after the surgery.

Johnson wished his hair had turned snow-white like Ted Danson's or Mike Pence's instead of the mottled gray he saw in the mirror each morning, then wondered why he even cared given no one else would. He wished his blue eyes looked more awake, more alert and focused, but again, there wasn't much to focus on, so why would they?

Cecile, Johnson's wife, had passed away just after their joint retirement at age 70. He had waited the five months for her age to catch up with his so they could jump into the retirement pool together, with a splash, holding hands, celebrating like kids, with no plans but to relish their new freedom. Then she fell from the ladder while clearing leaves from the gutters in the spring of that freedom, leaving Johnson alone with an emptiness he could not fathom.

***

Officer Upland appeared at Johnson's door on an evening in the early fall of Johnson's 76th year. Upland had acquired the nickname "Roundup" from his fellow officers because he was, in fact, quite round with short stout legs, protruding belly, no neck and a perfect ball for a head. His name didn't help, it being Rowen Upland, the butt of many puns through adolescence. He preferred "Roundup." It had a cowboy flair to it.

He took his hat off as he stood at the door and greeted his old captain by his title with a "Long time no see" and a smile.

"Roundup, good to see you. It's been quite a while!" Johnson exclaimed, excited to have a visitor of any sort.

"Yup. Your retirement party, I think."

"Come on in."

Roundup entered the living room, nervously tapping his hat against his leg.

"How are you? What brings you here tonight? Have a seat." Johnson beamed.

"I'm doing okay. Keeping busy with the same ole, same ole."

"I bet."

"We all didn't want to bother you about this, considering

everything, but we're dealing with a case that you might help us with. Sheriff thought we should talk to you."

Johnson again invited him to have a seat on the well-aged leather sofa.

"This won't take that long, Captain. It's about one of Cecile's best friends, Hilda Small. We're looking for some background on her, and Cecile being so close to her we thought you might have some insight. They were pretty close, right?"

"Yes, they were very close. You sure you don't want a seat? I'm gonna sit, if you don't mind. My left knee is acting up. So, what's going on with Hilda?" Johnson slowly lowered himself onto his rocking chair.

"She was found dead yesterday in her home, and the circumstances are a little suspicious. Not a lot, no signs of forced entry or another's presence, nothing suggesting an attack, just the surroundings a little weird."

Johnson was quiet for a moment, his eyes seeming to lose focus. "Suspicious? How?" he finally asked, his voice almost a whisper.

"You know she lived alone. Looks like she was involved with some kind of ritual at the time of her death. Her sister dropped by to visit yesterday afternoon. They had planned to go shopping together. Arranged it the day before. Found the door unlocked and Hilda in the kitchen slumped over the table."

Johnson was slow to respond. He had closed his eyes as Roundup spoke, and they slowly opened. "So, the ritual? Where does that come in?" he inquired quietly.

Roundup took a deep breath. "Here's the thing. The kitchen tablecloth was black. Not what you'd expect. Maybe a guy'd have one, but not an elderly lady. Don't ya think? Six candles were set in a circle in front of her. They had burned down into a pool of wax at the base of the candle holders. They must have been lit when she lost consciousness, which raises questions about what she was doing. There was a

75

string of beads in her left hand, like a rosary, but not. Black beads, no crucifix, but a black tassel hanging off. There were these small plastic cards, lots of 'em, with colorful circles and symbols. And weirdest of all, five teeth in an Altoids tin in her lap. We've seen weirder stuff, I guess. But this got me curious." Roundup paused. "Cause of death looks like maybe heart failure. The medical examiner is, you know, examining. Anyway, it's that paraphernalia on the table that's got me thinking maybe something weird was going on."

"Damn it, Roundup, sit down. Your hovering is driving me crazy." Johnson was alert now, his voice in command tone.

Roundup sat down on the sofa and set his hat on his knee.

"I've not kept much in touch with Hilda since Cecile passed," Johnson lied. "The two of them were very close, Cecile and Hilda, but I didn't pay much attention to their goings-on, working as I was so many hours. Cecile never mentioned anything about what you're talking about. After we both retired, they saw less of each other. Hilda was a bit of a recluse, kept to herself. Guess I'm not much help."

"Okay, that's fine. Thanks, Cap." As Roundup stood to leave, his hat slipped off his knee falling beside the end table at the sofa's arm. His eye caught a small bundle of cloth on the table, two rectangular pieces with colorful symbols, sitting on top of a lump of slim string like strands of what looked like cloth. It reminded him of the items on top of Hilda's kitchen table. His instinct was to ask Johnson what it was, but he was on his way out. It most likely didn't matter.

***

Alone now, Johnson rubbed his forehead. He could have told him the truth, that he and Hilda had seen a lot of each other since Cecile's death, almost weekly, playing mahjong

76

solitaire beside each other, talking about things insignificant and the insignificance of their lives. He had not seen her for a few days and now began to react physically to the news of her death. He struggled to raise himself from his chair, his left knee feeling particularly weak. Finally on his feet, he bent over the sofa's arm to reach the devotional scapular on the end table. His knee gave way, and he fell to the floor.

***

On his way back to the station Roundup couldn't stop thinking about the similarity of whatever that was on Johnson's table to whatever those plastic cards with strange symbols were on Hilda's. He wondered if it was worthy of further investigation, then thought that a foolish idea. He had no reason to doubt Johnson.

***

Johnson, on the other hand, now doubted himself. He did not know the man who had just lied to Roundup. It was the human frailty he had encountered and hated the most in his 30 years on the force. The "I wasn't speeding," "I didn't do it," "I have no idea what you're talking about" response in the face of overwhelming evidence to the contrary. His relationship with Hilda was an unexpected but natural sequel to his marriage. She had been widowed 10 years when Cecile died. He knew her—her quiet self-effacing strength, her gentle humor. And she knew him. She had consoled Johnson in his grief. He had felt particularly abandoned by Cecile's passing so early in their retirement and Hilda had offered him the companionship he was desperate to restore. Now Hilda was gone, and he was alone again. There was so much he could have told Roundup about Hilda, about her expansive soul that embraced the world's contradictions, her generosity, compassion and support. He had failed her by lying. He had

77

to redeem himself somehow. He knew exactly the what and the why about what had attracted Roundup's attention.

***

The next morning Roundup reported to the sheriff about his meeting with Johnson. "Pretty much a cipher, waste of time," he said. "Johnson didn't look too good. Not like 1 remembered him. He's lost a lot of weight. I was waiting for one of those awful jokes he used to tell, but he didn't deliver. He didn't even seem too surprised to hear of Hilda Small's death. I told him about that ritual thing. He had nothing to offer. I think it's a nothing burger. I'd say we still go with natural causes."

Roundup paused and took a deep breath. "I will say, though, that stuff on the table, the teeth in her lap, very strange."

"Okay, I'll check with the M.E. and see where she's at. I'll let you know," the sheriff replied. "You've got some other things to deal with, like Micky the missing turtle. You'd better get on it before he scampers further away."

***

At his desk, looking through his five open case files, the turtle case sat at the bottom of the pile below the break in at the Happy Hour, where nothing seemed to be missing, the broken car window on Sanchez Street, the loud, fisty argument that had spilled out into a cul- de-sac, and the Hilda Small death. Micky, the turtle, would have to wait. Roundup picked out the Small case to look at one more time. He was thinking about the sister who had found her dead. Did the sister say anything about the beads, or the candles or those cards of symbols? She had reported the death, had been alone with Hilda's body for some time, had called 911 and waited. It had taken at least ten minutes for them to respond.

78

What did she think about the scene? No one had asked.

Her name was Gertrude Leona. He found her phone number and punched it in, remembering her as slight, pale, blonde, probably in her sixties.

Gertrude Leona picked up on the first ring. "Bob?" she asked, an excited anticipation in her voice.

"Gertrude Leona?" Roundup asked, thinking he might have the wrong number.

"Who's this?"

"Officer Upland from the county sheriff's office. Is this Ms. Leona?"

"Not funny, Bob. Are you coming or not? I thought you'd be here by now!"

"Ms. Leona, this is officer Rowen Upland from the Sheriff's Office. Please accept my deepest sympathy in the loss of your sister. We met at your sister's house the other night. Is this a bad time? I have a few final questions. But they can wait if you're busy now. When would be good?"

"Good for what?"

"For a conversation about the circumstances of your sister's death - just a few questions. If you're expecting another call, if this is a bad time, it can wait."

"Wait for what?"

"Ms. Leona, are you all right?" Roundup hesitated a moment. Why was this so difficult? He was tensing up, a little irritated. "A better time to talk."

"About what?"

"The circumstances of Hilda's death." He paused, took a breath. "Know what? Could I pay you a visit? That might be easier. I caught you at a bad time. Will you be home this afternoon?"

"This afternoon?"

"Yes?"

"What about this afternoon?"

"Will you be home this afternoon? I'd like to drop by to talk to you."

"You would?"

"Yes, would that be all right?"

"About what? I thought you were Bob."

"I know. I could tell."

"How could you tell?

"You called me by his name."

"I called you Bob? You're not Bob. Who are you?"

"Officer Upland from the Monroe County Sheriff's Office. I'd like to talk to you about your sister if I could. Would that be all right? We could talk now on the phone or I could drop by your home this afternoon. Which would work best?"

"I thought you were Bob. You were supposed to be Bob. He's probably calling me right now and getting the busy signal." Gertrude Leona hung up.

***

Roundup put his head in his hands and willed himself to relax. He had to admit he was likely on a fool's errand of his own making, all because what he saw on Hilda's table and in her lap did not conform to his expectations for an elderly person's death of natural causes. He knew what to expect after so many similar cases, finding them in the bathroom or on the kitchen floor, or at the bottom of the stairs. The setting for this one was an anomaly he couldn't seem to ignore. Maybe he was making too much of it, and the crazy conversation with Gertrude Leona only confirmed it.

He raised his head, tried to rub the tension out of his round forehead, and immediately searched Hilda Small's file for Gertrude's address—15 Parkview Terrace, Irondequoit. His map app found the street off St. Paul Boulevard close to the shore of Lake Ontario, an area of mostly modest older cottage-like homes built in the '30s. He would definitely drop by that afternoon. He needed to know which of the two of them was crazy. This time he wouldn't call first.

The more Johnson thought about Hilda's death and

Roundup's visit, the more guilt he felt. He could easily have told him about the beads and the teeth and candles, about the mahjong tiles and the game and Hilda's belief that these talismans brought her support and success as she played. He had seen these harmless superstitions arrayed in front of bingo players all those nights he'd called numbers to raise money for local charities. Tiny toy hula dancers, cats, dogs, alligators, religious symbols, pictures of loved ones arrayed beside the game board, ensuring that winning numbers would be called for them. For Hilda it was the mahjong challenge that required supernatural intervention.

He could have told Roundup that he and Hilda played beside each other almost weekly, that he had begged off the night she died to nurse his aches and pains, that had he been there he might have saved her life, would have saved her life, called for help immediately; he had the training, had saved lives before as a first responder.

The day after Roundup's visit Johnson was so distracted by his guilt that he could concentrate on nothing else. He needed to man-up but feared the loss of the respect he enjoyed with his old colleagues after all his positive and self-less work over the years. What was a man's life without his good name and the reputation he had earned?

***

Roundup walked up the front steps to the broad screened-in porch across the front of Gertrude's house. It was weathered from its year's lake side, from the notorious lake-effect snow, the scavenging gulls, the wind off the water. He tested the floorboards each step to the door. He didn't know what to expect, given the phone call. He was in uniform. He presumed she would remember him.

"Who are you and what do you want?" were Gertrude's first words while opening the door.

"Officer Upland. We spoke this morning concerning your

81

sister's death. We met at her house the other night, the night you found her and called it in. I just have a few more questions."

"You're black. I remember you, the black officer."

"Yes, the same one. Do you want to talk here on the porch or inside?"

She was wearing a simple soft green housedress that hung loosely over her sleight frame, and the two together made a picture of contrasts. "Did you see Bob out there before you came in? He's supposed to be cleaning up the yard. He was late again, only just got here. I need his help, as much as I don't. Get it?"

Roundup thought he saw a smile flicker across her thin lips, but her cold eyes drew his attention away from them. This is a very strange woman, he thought. "I'll get right to the point. When you found your sister, she was in a chair, her body slumped over the kitchen table. That's how we found her when we got to the scene. Do you know anything about what was on her kitchen table - you know, the beads and candles and the cards with the colorful circles and symbols? We also found a tin with teeth in it in her lap. Does any of that mean anything to you?"

She looked directly into his eyes. "Are there many black men on the police force?" she asked.

"There are a quite a few of us, yes. Men and women."

"Oh."

"About my question. Do you remember those things I mentioned?"

"What things?"

"You know, the beads, the candles, the stuff on your sister's kitchen table."

"Do I remember them? I Just saw Bob out the window. He's raking up those leaves, so many leaves. It'll take him forever the rate he's going."

Roundup decided to approach her from a different angle. "Ms. Leona, how often did you see your sister? Visit with her?"

"Hilda or the other one?"

"Hilda. The one you called us about the other night."

"We were going to go shopping together, but we didn't."

"Yes, that's what you told us. Is that something you did often together?"

"I hate shopping. Most of the time I can't find what I want."

"I hate it too." He wanted to access her confidence, but Roundup was getting as frustrated with this conversation as he did with the earlier phone call. Still, he was insistent. "Back to the other night, why were there candles on her table?"

"It was the damned mahjong, the candles, the beads"

"What was?"

"She never wanted to go shopping with me. She always had to be playing that stupid game. Day and night, it seemed. She tried to teach me how to play it, said I could play it with her. Wasn't anything I wanted to do."

"The candles were about the game. Is that what you're saying? It's called what? Mahjong?"

"Mahjong," she repeated. "Just because you have your wisdom teeth doesn't make you any smarter. Let alone your baby teeth. They'd make you dumber, don't you think?"

"Is the game the cards with the symbols?"

"Tiles."

"What?"

"They aren't cards, they're tiles. Just saw Bob again."

Roundup turned to where she was looking, a wall with no windows, a few large family photos hanging.

"Where?" Roundup asked. "Where did you see Bob?"

"Right there," she answered, pointing to the largest of the framed photos which appeared to be of a picnic gathering.

"In the picture, you mean? You saw Bob in the picture?"

"He should be raking leaves. That's what I asked him over to do."

83

Roundup took a deep breath. He had been standing in front of Gertrude Leona, three feet away from her, for what seemed like forever. His short, substantial legs had stiffened, and his back had tensed as his frustration grew. He decided to make one last effort with the three words he'd written on his pad—candles, mahjong, tiles. "Ms. Leona, you think the beads and the teeth had something to do with the game?"

"What game?"

"Mahjong. It's a game, right?"

"For Hilda, everything had to do with the game. I could never figure it out. Confused the hell out of me. Took concentration, she'd say. I'd rather not."

"Rather not what?"

"Concentrate. Too much work. You want to meet Bob? Let's go out and find him. He's probably napping in the hammock out back." She took his hand and led him out the door. There was no one in the yard.

***

Back at the office Roundup called Johnson. "Hey Captain, enjoyed seeing you last night. Just wanted you to know I figured out what all that paraphernalia was on Hilda Small's kitchen table. She was playing mahjong and it all had something to do with that. Like lucky charms. Mystery solved. We're all set here with natural causes. You have a nice evening."

"You too," Johnson replied softly. "And call again if you think I could be of any help with cases in the future." With this lie, Johnson, able to relax for the first time in 24 hours, was suddenly awashed with grief over Hilda's death.

Rumor, Truth or Lie

A lie is the ninth thou shalt not,
The tug that loosens the knot,
The crack in the bell
That chimes all is well,
The wet that inhabits the rot.

A truth is a slug in the mud
Or the stone that drops with a thud
Or a bird that sings
The first notes of spring
Or the love that blesses a hug.

A rumor can be truth or lie,
Its purpose to shine a dark light
On something hidden
Without permission,
Designed to hurt or surprise.

A rumor is quite like a tumor
That grows large and then much firmer,
Caressed by cruel spite
Or damning insight
Far from discerning observers.

A rumor, a truth and a lie
Sat in a bar drinking rye.
Their knuckles were bruised,
Their eyes black and blue
From the fight they'd just had outside.

The fight was about which was worse -
The rumor, the lie, or truth's curse.
When they couldn't agree,
With no referee,
The vitriol grew and then burst.

For there's no evaluation,
Math, or discrimination
That can weigh the pain
And actually name
Degrees of excruciation

Of the hurt when you are lied to
Or from false rumors about you,
Or truth in the dark
Lit up by a spark
Of a revelation that burns you.

Rumor, Truth or Lie

"Let's play truth or lie," he said. "I'll get the whiskey." He got up from the kitchen table and walked to the cupboard, a tall, broad-shouldered man in his early thirties. He squeezed the bottle into his arm pit, took a shot glass in each hand and walked into the living room. With the bottle in the middle of the coffee table and a glass on either side, he sat at one end of the sofa and patted the cushion on the other. "We're all set here," he said, as if there were others in the room.

She was still in the kitchen putting the dishes away. "What's the big hurry?" she asked. "Give me a minute." He watched her from the sofa as she lifted the freshly cleaned plates into the cupboard above her head. "You know you could at least do this part." She was a thin woman, wearing a sports jersey and green tights.

"I could," he said, "but I'd rather watch the way your butt moves in those tights when you put those away."

Her blonde hair fell to the back of her shoulders as she looked up and reached for the shelf. The plates in place, she slowly turned to him. "Pour me a shot," she said. "I'll be there in a minute."

Truth or lie was their before-foreplay. A game that typically ended in the bedroom, it was a vestige of their first date. That winter night he was hoping for just a " thank you for a good time" kiss at the door to her apartment, but she had invited him in to get warm before his walk to the subway, offered him a shot, and a way to enhance it. "Truth or lie?" she had asked. "Don't guess the lie and take a drink. Guess the lie and win the kiss."

This night he brushed his black hair back off his forehead, poured her shot and one for himself. In the two years since that first night, each had learned to manipulate the game: the more obvious the lie, the more likely the kiss; the less obvious, the more likely a buzz.

She returned and sat beside him, facing away, out toward the kitchen, her blue eyes closed, her face like the Virgin Mary's, not luminous or beatific, but with those soft features in that perfect oval.

"You really want to play this game tonight?" she asked.

"Sure, don't you?"

"I don't know," she answered, turning her head to face him.

Mixed signals. He didn't know how to respond. She had asked for the drink. She knew the set up. Why didn't she just say "no" in the first place?

"I don't know," she said again and took a deep breath. More like a sigh. "Maybe I do."

"Something the matter with your lie radar tonight?" he asked. "Not feelin' confident? You know we both win in the end. Always have."

She toyed with the full shot glass for a moment, then took a sip.

***

"You just broke the rules. No drinking before the game begins. You must want to lose," he said. There was disappointment in his voice.

"I get to start, okay?" she asked.

"I think you already have," he joked half-heartedly.

She didn't smile. She took another sip of whiskey. "Okay, here goes. I'm in my thirty-second year of life. My mom lives in Queens. I have blue eyes."

Had her mother moved? If she hadn't, he believed all

three statements were true. There being no lie, he would lose. No kiss. Her mom must have moved, he thought, otherwise she was cheating. "One of those statements has to be a lie," he reminded her.

"Right. Which is it?" she asked.

"I know you're thirty-two, that your eyes are blue. So, your mother must have moved. Why didn't you tell me?"

"Wrong. I'm in my thirty-third year of life, not the thirty-second."

"What?"

"When I turned thirty-two, I had lived thirty-two years. I've lived beyond that now. I'm in my thirty-third year of life. Just like when from birth to one I was in my first year, before I turned one. Then I was in the second year of my life. Get it? I thought you were a college graduate. Drink it down, boy!"

He looked for her smile. It wasn't there. He drank the shot and filled his glass.

"Are you ready?" he asked.

She nodded that she was. "Okay, which one's the lie? I was eight when I caught my first fish. It was a bluegill. I was fishing with my dad in Black Lake." He had told her the story a number of times. It was a significant moment in his life. He grew up with a voracious appetite for fishing after that first fish. But she wasn't sure of his exact age or of the kind of fish on that momentous day. Bluegill didn't sound right. Like he made it up. It didn't even register for her as a type of fish. But the mention of Black Lake took her back to their car ride to upstate New York when he showed her the fishing camp on Black Lake. They sat on the dock and dangled their feet in the very green water. The incongruity of the algae and milfoil infestation with the lake's name had left an impression. She didn't want to get the right answer. She didn't want the kiss.

"There's no lake by that name," she said

"What?" It was almost a shout. "How can you say that? I even took you to the lake. What's going on? If you just want to drink, we don't have to play this game." He was angry, more at her apparent disregard for a significant event his life, than at the obvious lie she had told.

She emptied her shot glass. "My turn," she said quickly. "You ready? You recovered?"

"Yeah, I'm ready," he answered, his disappointment a shadow beside his words.

"Okay, good, two truths and a lie coming your way. Which one's the lie? You are stalking Karen Webster. You're sleeping with Karen Webster. There's a rumor at your office that you're obsessed with Karen Webster. Which one's the lie?"

He was stunned. Didn't know what to say. She was looking directly into his eyes. He couldn't look into hers. The statements were supposed to be about her, not him, that was their rule, so that's what he said, the words stumbling out of his mouth. "They're supposed to be about you. The truths and lies."

She moved her face closer to his. Her voice was steady. "They are about me, James. Don't you get it? All three. Tell me. Which one's the lie?

Snake

A desert snake from Oued Zem
Could not shed his aging skin.
His body would grow,
His skin would just hold,
Unable to free his distention.

He crawled to a charmer nearby
Who played on his pungi a while.
Tho' he thought that it would,
It did him no good
And he slithered away and he cried.

As the skin on his face constricted,
He became more dispirited.
His eyes like a bug's
Slimed like a slug's,
Wept with cold tears unrestricted.

A snake named F'atima slinked near
And seeing this sad snake in tears
Slid up by his side,
Looked in his eyes,
Asked "What is the matter, my dear?"

The snake from the desert explained.
She listened and curled 'round his frame.
Her tongue was unleashed,
Receptive to seek
A way that would end this cruel pain.

"One must do some things for one's self
When things don't occur we expect.
A cure you must choose
To cut the skin loose
And set yourself free from its threat.

Don't martyr yourself to this plight.
Don't surrender, put up a fight.
If you tear the skin
At one of its ends,
You might free your old skin tonight."

He knew it would cost him some pain.
A small price to pay, he'd explain.
He looked for sharp stones
Or jagged-edged bones
To crawl on again and again.

With F'atima beside him that night,
He labored with all of his might.
At the edge of stone steps
He could not quite detect
He tumbled down out of her sight.

Twenty feet to the ground below
With nothing to cushion the blow,
His serpentine heap
Lay in the street
Cast in the sun's early glow.

Is this where this story should end -
One more martyr in Oued Zem
Losing the fight
He fought this night
Just to bend to nature's cold whim?

Thu'ban

Thu'ban, a desert horned viper, had fallen clumsily off the stone steps. As he painfully unwound himself beside the bottom step, he was dizzy and disoriented. He was also lost. He thought he knew the city well, but as he looked about, he could find no familiar landmark. Maybe it was because he had hit his head. If he just waited awhile, he thought, the world as he knew it would come back into focus. And wasn't there another snake with him before the fall? He couldn't remember.

He believed he felt a loosening of the skin around his neck, his beautiful skin with its patterns in brown and yellow. Could it be that the shedding had begun? He slithered forward to test if he was leaving the old skin behind, but turning his head back to look, he felt the same painful tightening around his face. Even the fall hadn't helped. He'd never heard of such a thing. The shedding had always been a regular and painless event that revealed a more glistening version of himself.

***

He slid forward to get a better view of his location. He assumed he was somewhere in the city's outskirts, where he typically spent hours each day under the loose sand, waiting to strike a passing lizard or frog for lunch. But what he could see was strange to him and discomfiting. He thought a more

94

elevated view might help, but the idea of navigating back up those stone steps frightened him. He decided to wait until his head cleared before trying to find his way home. Slithering back to the dark corner of the bottom step, Thu'ban curled up and fell asleep.

Vague images drifted through his dreams—snakes coiling themselves around each other, lizards escaping his fangs, a cool night and a bright moon, a charmer's swaying, silent pungi.

A sudden sensation at the back of his head grew from a vague pressure to a sharp pain that jarred him awake. His eyes opened upon the sunburned feet of a man. Thu'ban's head was suddenly lifted into the air, his eyes now scanning the sky, his body flailing in the day's heat. Almost as suddenly, he dropped into a woven basket. Shut in, he wriggled and thrashed for a way to escape, and felt the skin behind his eyes break free.

The irony of shedding his skin while encased in a wicker prison was not lost on Thu'ban. One oppression traded for another, he thought. He knew exactly what had happened. Many times he had witnessed snake charmers hunting his fellow vipers. With their forked sticks in hand, they lingered around possible snake holes for a viper to emerge and jammed the fork around its neck. Lifting the snake high into the air made the lethal fangs useless and wriggling free pointless. Dropped into a basket or a canvas pouch, the viper would disappear from Thu'ban's world.

He had also seen the end result—listless snakes lifting their heads out of the open wicker baskets in front of the charmers, swaying to the movement of the pungi, pretending they could hear the music, wanting only to embed their poisoned fangs into the charmer, but too far away and too weak to strike. They always looked so sick and close to death. Thu'ban had seen many charmers spill their dead snakes onto the ground and kick them to the edge of the square. This was not an end he wanted for himself.

***

He felt the sway of the basket he rode as the charmer walked. If Thu'ban was dizzy before, he was now nauseous. The dark, cramped space was stiflingly hot. It was impossible to straighten out or comfortably arrange his aching body. A future as a charmer's slave was frightening. He fell into a swoon, a foggy mental miasma of helplessness and grief. Consciousness of his body's discomfort seemed to fall away as a cry for submission welled up from behind his eyes, a plea to accept this fate. There was little recourse in the face of this greater power as he felt his strength and will slip away.

Then suddenly, as if erupting from his dispassion, an explosion of shock rattled his body, eclipsing all else, as startling as the fall from the stone steps. Stabs of bright pain stuttered down his length, which was now flopping along the ground.

Finally lying still, he saw the lid of the basket beside him. The basket itself had disappeared. Thu'ban struggled to catch his breath. What had just happened, he wondered. Where was the charmer? Was he free?

As he tried to orient himself, Fátima slithered to his side. "Thu'ban," she said. "Thu'ban, I bit him in the foot. I tracked him and bit him in the foot. Can you crawl? We need to get away! We are too much in the open. Can you follow me? You must follow me!"

"Yes, yes, show me the way, please, show me the way," Thu'ban cried, lifting his head to meet her eyes.

Elliptical

Considering Vygotsky's realm
Of proximal development,
The theorist claimed
That learning came
From varied social stimulants.

Considering proximity,
The moon's sea of tranquility
Too far away
To reach, they'd say,
Without extreme audacity.

Consider please the moon and stars,
Where life might be, just like ours,
In houses built
Of bones and silk
From hopes and dreams of avatars.

Consider life a passing phase.
The spirit's journey, some would say.
What comes before
And follows soars
Above the existential plane.

Considering the journey's arc
The glow from that initial spark
Liftoff, star-ship,
Flat line, round trip,
Transcendence when we disembark.

Considering that early glow,
A beaming from a source unknown
The light of fate?
A god's bright ray?
Evolution's blinding eros?

What is the source of what is true?
Instinct or our social milieu?
Vygotsky'd say
It's clear as day:
It's thoughts that track 'tween you and you.

Rupert Longjohn

He said he preferred the Socratic method, rather than a more straight-forward exposition. Let understanding be an act of discovery. Let the shell of an idea lead you to the kernel, the nut cracking open to reveal a truth. It's the law school approach, he would say.

But this wasn't law school. It was a high school sophomore literature class and the challenge was finding that opening question, the one that would lead to the next and then the next until the answer to the last hit on a significant truth. So he began his discussion of The Scarlet Letter with Pearl, the illegitimate daughter in Hawthorne's classic, and what her presence and behavior meant. They had read the book, knew the story. His first question: "How does an oyster create a pearl?"

***

It made sense to him to use the Socratic method in his personal life as well. It was how he enabled conversations. He was an introvert who didn't have the gift of gab, that hail- fellow-well-met gene. He discovered that this dialogic technique helped him through conversations in uncomfortable settings. He always hoped that the answer to the first question he would ask would contain the seed of a follow-up question to keep the conversation going until he could extract himself. When it didn't, he was helplessly speechless.

He was shy with adults, but not with his students. They

didn't intimidate him. It was any adult he didn't know and any adult in a professional position of greater distinction than a public school teacher that frightened him. In fact, he questioned if public school teachers were professionals. They were certainly not of the same stature as a college professor or lawyer or doctor. Teachers were just one rung up from vocational. If you do the math, he'd say, given the time spent nights and weekends preparing, the hourly rate deflated like a flat tire.

It was the thread and weave of his dialogues with students that engaged him and stoked his enthusiasm for teaching. He remembered his high school American history teacher who would lecture while writing an outline of her lecture on the blackboard, with names and dates and abbreviated phrases noting significance. She might embellish the facts with a quick story or an historical individual's profile, but beyond that, it was just a chart on a black board that he copied into his notebook to remember as best he could for the next test. It was boring. He spent most of the class tallying the number of times she asked "OK?" with each statement of fact, over two hundred some days.

He remembered his English literature teacher who had a story to tell about every author they read. Again, no give-and-take, no "What do you think?", no personal engagement about the work. Rupert remembered how he wept when he read the conclusion of *A Tale of Two Cities,* how the tears surprised him, and how he wanted them to stop when they would not. He wanted to understand why, but saw no path to a conversation with his teacher about his unexpected reaction.

His name was Rupert Longjohn, appropriately tall and thin, his wild hair like a disturbed bird's nest. He taught standing in front of the class, towering over the students, scanning the class through his wire-rimmed glasses. He began the year looking for any student with a raised hand, willing to answer his questions. With each answer he'd ask

100

what the others thought and look for a different hand waving to respond. In this way he moved the conversation around the room from one student to another. The eager students were the brave few, but Rupert wanted all to be involved. So after the first weeks his approach changed. Ignoring the raised hands, he would choose to lead an unsuspecting student through a series of questions to reach that revelatory moment- the answer he sought. Initially he'd call on students who had willingly engaged in the past, believing they were the most comfortable with his interrogations and could serve as an example for the shy, quiet ones that there was nothing to fear.

Some students were terribly anxious about his approach, did not want to be singled out to enter his web of inquiry, even though the experience for those who did always appeared to end with a surprising insight, a prideful moment of relief, and praise. He empathized with the reluctant students, acknowledging his own self-conscious reaction as a high school student on those occasions when he had been singled out to answer a question in front of the class.

It wasn't until a chilly November day that Rupert decided he would engage with Theresa, the obviously shy student who discreetly sat in the back corner of the classroom, slouched down to the degree that if the teacher was not as tall as Rupert Longjohn, she would have been invisible. Rupert assumed her posture a lack of confidence, a reflection of his own teenage insecurity. He would tread carefully, lob a softball question, and give her ample time to reflect. He had chosen what he considered a short Wallace Stevens poem, "Metaphors of a Magnifico," for her initiation.

"Theresa," he began, "how are you this morning?"

"Fine," she said quietly, clearly surprised to be called on. She lifted her head, brushed her bangs aside, and straightened her posture, her large blue eyes opening wide.

"You've read the poem." It was a statement of fact, not a question.

"Yes," she replied, a rough edge to the word.

Rupert noticed the Red Cross pin on the collar of her blouse. "You support the Red Cross, I see. Do you volunteer?"

"Yes," she answered. Her cheeks had flushed. One hand had curled into a fist.

"That must be very rewarding."

"Yes."

"I'm sure it is. Why don't you read the poem aloud to the class."

Theresa bowed her head toward the hand-out. Her voice barely audible, she read the poem.

"Twenty men crossing a bridge,
Into a village
Are twenty men crossing twenty bridges,
Into twenty villages,
Or one man
Crossing a single bridge into a village

This is old song

That will not declare itself...

Twenty men crossing a bridge,
Into a village,
Are
Twenty men crossing a bridge
Into a village.

That will not declare itself
Yet is as certain as meaning...

The boots of the men clump
On the boards of the bridge.
The first white wall of the village
Rises through fruit-trees.
Or what was it I thinking?

So the meaning escapes.

The first white wall of the village...
The fruit-trees..."

Theresa looked up at Rupert, relieved to have finished the reading, surprised it had ended so abruptly.

"Let's begin, then, shall we, Theresa? What is a metaphor?" Rupert asked.

Theresa did not respond.

Rupert waited a moment. "Theresa?" He waited again, then asked, "Do I need to repeat the question?"

"What is a metaphor," she said, more a statement, as if she were repeating the question to herself. "We all know what a metaphor is. You've told us before, many times," she continued, her tone suggesting irritation. "It says one thing is something else. What's a magnifico?"

Rupert was surprised by the question. It was his job to pose the questions he'd mapped out to reach his target destination, the moment of revelation. Rupert responded with his chosen pedagogy. "Let's ask someone else." He looked around the room. "Roger, what's a magnifico?"

"I don't know. It doesn't say in the poem," the boy answered.

"Anybody? Does anybody know?" Rupert asked. Finding no volunteers, he answered. "I believe a magnifico is a very important person."

Theresa raised her hand. "I don't understand. What does a very important person have to do with this poem? I don't see the connection. You've got all these guys walking across

103

a bridge, twenty guys walking across a bridge into a town, I guess. Or one. I don't know, which is it? Where is there anything in the poem about an important person?"

The students were searching the hand out in front of them for evidence of the magnifico, for something that would suggest a definition.

This was not the direction he wanted the dialogue to go. He wanted them to uncover the magnifico's role. But the moment demanded his intervention. "The magnifico is implied to be the observer. The implication is drawn from the title that he is the person observing the men walking across the bridge."

"So, the title is part of the poem, the first line of the poem?" Theresa asked. "How would we know that?"

A boy in the front row raised his hand. "We wouldn't," he blurted. "Don't we have to ignore the title and just talk about the lines of the poem? I don't see any metaphors that make any sense. How can twenty men be one guy? And one bridge twenty bridges and one village twenty villages. It's like the magnifico guy is on drugs." The class broke into laughter.

"He's hallucinating," a student shouted. "He's buzzed out."

"What's the song, the old song?" another asked. "Are they singing? It doesn't say they're singing."

"How does a song declare itself? What does that even mean?" yet another asked. "Isn't that personification?"

"Or he's dreaming," from another.

"Who's 'he'?" someone asked. "Who's hallucinating?"

The magnifico, Theresa thought to herself. *The magnifico is hallucinating.* So she said it, her voice louder than the others. "It's like he's thinking of something else because of what he's seeing. He's in his head. He can't get out of his head. See, at the end, he can't even remember why he's thinking about it. It's all part of the same picture in his head."

"Yes," Rupert said, excitedly."Yes. When we look at something, is it just what we see, or does it also represent something else, something else it could be? Can someone give me another example?"

Confuse

Don't confuse the shiv with the shank
Or confound the slap with the spank.
A difference lies
'Neath the foggy guise
Of similarity's pranks.

Those words where the difference is slight
Can quite naturally incite
Misunderstanding
Or anger landing
On those who don't know what's right.

Are ethos and ethics the same?
Is my ache the same as your pain?
Did you mean to confuse
Or set up a ruse
To have an advantage for gain?

And what is the point of all this?
That words can't be just hit-or-miss?
Forget what I said,
I meant this instead,
And ask for your forgiveness.

Is It Perspicuity or Perspicacity?

"This is what I don't understand," she said, leaning in toward the woman's face across from her, elbows on the table, chin in the cup of her palms. "Tao is a belief there is a natural order to the universe that we can't perceive, a rational order that we can't see. That's what you're telling me, right?"

"Yes," the professor answered as she slid herself to the back of the booth, away from the face of the young woman who struggled to understand. "Yes, it is something you can only intuit from experience."

"Is the natural order you intuit the same as the one I do?" the student asked, her brow wrinkled, her eyes squinting.

"We each experience life differently, so I suppose not."

"So, the answer is no. That's what you're saying. The natural order of the universe would be different for each of us. How can that be?"

"Angela, to be clear, Taoism is a path to wisdom, not the understanding that wisdom brings."

"Oh my, now you tell me it's a path and not that other thing, the natural order thing."

The professor took a sip of her coffee, collected her thoughts. She knew the struggle her young student was having, had seen it many times before. She wanted to help. "I know this is difficult. Have you ever heard the expression 'the willing suspension of disbelief' that describes the way we typically approach a magician or a movie like "Ghost Busters" or stories about the super-natural? We want to believe the premise is true so we can enjoy the experience even though we know it isn't true. Think of Taoism that way."

"Like magical thinking?" Angela exclaimed, excited to be able to contribute. "Like if we can think it, or imagine it, we can believe it's real? I get it now." Angela's shoulders sagged as she pulled her elbows off the table, her chin from her palms.

***

She lied. She didn't get it, didn't get what she wanted - a natural, rational order to the universe that made sense, that she could rely on, could fit herself into. She was looking for structure to hold herself together. That was why she took the class. She didn't want magical thinking; imagining didn't make something real.

Angela Weymouth was curious about the Tao philosophy because at her aunt's yoga class the instructor kept referring to it. "Go with the flow," the instructor would quietly repeat in a melodic cadence. "Wu wei, wu wei, feel the harmony of life itself." At the beginning of each session the instructor reminded the group that yoga would help them meld the personal with the universal, discover the harmony of mind and body, unite their human selves with all of nature, and free themselves from the chains of confusion to control their own destiny. Angela had yet to experience the epiphany.

There was the matter of her loneliness, brought on by her recent move away from home. At 19 years old she had run from her family, home-town, and an abusive, controlling boyfriend to the other side of the county to live with her aunt and uncle in Maine and clerk in their True Value hardware store. There was also the matter of her unfulfilled aspirations—an enjoyable job, a college education, a loving relationship, a family of her own. And the matter of the emotional challenges that starved her of any clear-eyed perspective on her own worth.

The Asian philosophy course had called out to her from the state university's continuing education brochure on the hardware store counter. With idle time each day waiting for customers, she thumbed through it often, always returning to that one course description that resonated for her. Maybe there was something to it, she had thought. Maybe this could make sense of things for her.

Angela looked young for her 19 years. Her round face, soft features, naturally curly blonde hair and slight frame suggested a still-budding teenager. The boyfriend experience had been so unexpected and unnerving, a transformation from unrelenting affection to physical abuse during her senior year in high school that sent her emotional compass into a painful, relentless spin. Unable to escape him and focus, she had abandoned the college search, jettisoned her friends, quit the only job she could find after graduation, and fought with her parents, whose expectations for her had been shattered.

It was her parents who suggested the move to Maine, to Uncle Jack and Aunt Cora's farm nestled in the wooded hills 20 miles from their store. Her parents fondly remembered their visit to Maine one autumn week 20 years earlier when Angela's birth was two months away. The sweet smell of the freshly hayed fields, the crisp blushing apples that burst bright nectar with each bite, and the profoundly quiet dark nights that fostered deep sleep. The visit had refreshed their senses and restored their equilibrium as they anxiously anticipated their first child. This, they thought, was exactly what Angela needed now.

Uncle Jack and Aunt Cora were a portrait of extremes— he a large, square, sturdy man with broad hips, shoulders and forehead, deep-set eyes and a smattering of gray hair, and Aunt Cora a diminutive woman whose blue eyes focused her attention on every moment of the day. What they had in common was a generous affability and a thoughtful approach to life.

At first the abrupt change focused Angela's attention outward, as she adjusted to the unfamiliar—Jack and Cora's unassuming genuine hospitality, the farm and the hardware store. It took a month for her to feel comfortable enough to assess her new life and consider its future. Short term on the East Coast, she thought. At most a year.

Uncle Jack asked her to help with the farm chores. Aunt Cora expected her assistance with household matters, and for Angela to accompany her to her weekly yoga. Routines were established that leveled her emotional landscape and allowed for exploration beyond its borders.

The six-week philosophy course that began mid-October was Angela's first foray into the world beyond the farm and store. As she drove to the university those evenings, she was amazed at the autumnal blanket of reds and yellows that covered the woods and hills hugging the roadside. The stunning beauty of the natural world bathed in the light of the setting sun validated her search for the core of universal symmetry suggested by the seasonal quarters of a year, the mantra of the yogi, and the spirit of the Taoism that she was studying. Three weeks into the course, confused and unsatisfied, she had met with the professor for coffee in the student union to find clarity. She was disappointed to learn that it was all a fiction, made up by searchers like herself, to explain the inexplicable.

***

"I thank God you're here," Cora Weymouth said, as she and Angela sat at the kitchen table peeling apples for a pie. "Truth be told, the store hasn't been doing too well and your uncle had to lay off the part-time boy and was working seven days a week. He was exhausted and hell to live with. Now, with you being there, he can breathe a little bit and so can I. It was like the days when we started out. He can't work like that at his age." Angela set down her paring knife and reached for an apple to eat. "It's enough to do to tend to the farm," Cora continued. "You missed the last of the haying, but we were both out there along with Jasper Frank down the road, working 'til sundown." Cora paused and looked out the kitchen window. "Your momma's call was a blessing. You want to help with the crust?"

"Sure, is it time?" Angela asked.

"Sure is," Cora said, on her feet now, heading to the pantry. "Done this before?"

"No," Angela replied and tried to imagine her aunt, tiny and thin, lugging hay bales in the rolling field behind the house. "All that hay in the barn, is that what you're talking about? There must be a couple hundred bales."

"That's right," Cora answered, back at the table with the flour, salt, and shortening. "Grab that bowl on the counter, will you?"

Angela watched her aunt mix the ingredients together, noticing for the first time the wrinkles and liver spots on her arms and small hands, the rough fingernails. She looked down at her own hands, soft, untested, resting on the table. "What if you didn't hay the field? Do you really need all that hay?"

"We sell the hay, honey. Every dollar counts. Even so, if we didn't tend to the field—spread the manure each spring, keep her green, cut her back—and just let her go, we'd get that rag weed, prickly pear, night shade, stinging nettle, and poison ivy, and have to plow it all under and start fresh. We used it as pasture for beef cows some years ago and they spread noxious weeds all over the seven acres. That was the last time we did that. Isn't that much money in beef cows anyway, and they kept getting out. We're done here for a while. Want a lemonade?"

***

A week later the water stopped, only a thin, weak stream from an open faucet. Cora was quick to explain. "The water pipe's clogged at the spring. We'll wait for your uncle to come home after work. I called him about it. This happens every fall. He's got the cure to it. You can use the outhouse in the shed, if you need to, or we can go without flushing 'til he gets home. We'll use the dug well beside the house if we need to for cooking. Just don't try to run the water, 'cause it can stop whatever siphon's left."

It was Angela's day off. She was supposed to spend some time studying the True Value inventory on those days, not just where the items were located but what they were for, so she could answer questions and prescribe, if necessary. She didn't know what it meant to lose a siphon. Just one more mystery, she thought. She'd wait for Uncle Jack to find out.

***

That evening, with the sun setting and Uncle Jack just home from the store, he asked Angela to help him restore the water. He led her though the connected shed into the barn and grabbed two lanterns. "It's getting dark. We'll need these to see what we're doing," he said. "Be nice if there was some kind of moon tonight, but I guess not." Jack donned a pair of high rubber boots he kept against a stall wall.

They walked across the front lawn to the farm road that led up the hill beside the back pasture. Leaves covered their path, hiding rocks and roots; trees shaded their way from any residual light. "Walk behind me, keep your lantern lighting the path, step high or you'll fall on your face," Jack warned. "We've got about 700 paces to go to the spring. Done this so many times I counted them so I'd know where to start looking for the damn thing in the dark. We got a pipe runs from the spring up here to the house, gravity feed. Before electricity and pumps, the water would run year 'round, from the spring down to the house into the kitchen, then out to that wooden barrel in the barn for the animals. Hundreds of feet of pipe under the pasture. Pretty ingenious, if you think about it. Water'd run year-round, under the frost line, then through the house. Love the idea. Now we got a pump. But leaves still clog it up and shut it down to a trickle, so we just got to clean it out at the source."

Angela shivered from the evening chill. *Why can't this wait for morning? she wondered. Why does he need me for this? Would Aunt Cora be with him if she wasn't?* Maybe that was it.

She stumbled on a rock and felt her ankle twist, a slight pain slicing through her foot. She shook it off. "Almost there," Jack said, turning his head back to check on her. "You okay?"

He abruptly stopped and turned to face her. "You been up here before this?"

"No," she answered quietly.

He pointed to the trees to the right of the road, opposite the pasture fence. "Cast your light over there. What do you see?" Her eyes followed the beam between the trees. It lit up a gravestone. "Let's go over there for a minute."

Behind a stand of white birch lay a small cemetery. Its gravestones, partly shrouded by tall grass, leaned forward or back, at odd, awkward angles to each other and the earth. "This farm dates back to the mid-1800's," Jack began. "No tractors, just horsepower. No furnace, just wood stoves and fireplaces. No refrigerator, just an ice box. No chain saws, just axes and hand saws. When I come up here I take a moment to thank those farmers for this place, let them know I appreciate their hard work and ingenuity and wisdom, let them know I'll take good care of the house and land, won't let them down." Jack's lantern swept over each row of graves to finally shed its light on Angela. "Ready? Let's get at it," he said, a touch of resignation in his voice.

***

114

A few minutes later Jack stopped at a break in the tree line, turned toward the pasture and cast his lantern's light down on a swarm of wet leaves hugging a small pool of water beneath them. "This is it," he said. "I'm gonna climb down in there and clean her out. I need you to light me up, okay? This won't take long. Just got to get them leaves out and away from the pipe for now. They're lodged in the screen covering the aperture. You still with me?"

Angela cast her light on the pool as Jack got down on all fours and tested for the pool's lip with his hands. Then, his elbows hugging the earth, he swung himself around, dropping his legs through the web of wet leaves. "Damn cold, damn cold." He shuddered.

Suddenly Angela worried for him as he bent forward so his hand could probe deep into the spring, down its earth wall to where the pipe lay below. Along the way he extended his free arm and swept up the leaves on the surface, drew them to him and heaved them toward the pasture. Angela's light flashed off the dark water. With a few wide strokes, the surface was cleared. "Now the fun part." Jack's voice was crusty and cold. He dropped his shoulder and reached deep, his face twisting away from the cold water that now tickled his ear. Slowly twigs and stems and leaves like translucent skins floated to the surface around him, wobbling on the ripples and clinging to his flannel collar.

"You need to get out of there, Uncle Jack, please," Angela pleaded.

"Yep, we're pretty much done here for now," he said, collecting the organic matter in his free hand and throwing it off toward the pasture fence. "Can you help me up?"

Angela moved toward him, leaned over and extended her hand, not considering the ratio of her strength and size to his. With his grasp's pull, her feet suddenly slid to the water's edge where she slipped, falling backward to the earth behind her, the lantern flying from her other hand.

"Oh my, Angela, you all right?" he called out as he

grabbed an exposed root near her foot and clumsily pulled himself from the pool.

Turning herself over and struggling to her knees, she looked up to see him standing beside her. "Let's get back to the house and the wood stove," he said as he helped her to her feet. "That's enough fun for tonight. These boots aren't much good when you're underwater. Need to get out of 'em. Tomorrow morning, before you come to work, could you take the steel rake in the shed, come back up here, and get as many of them leaves as you can out of the spring? I gotta be in real early for a delivery."

"Of course," Angela said to his broad back as they hurried down the path to the farmhouse.

***

The next morning Angela found a frost had settled over the ground during the night as she stepped from the woodshed to retrace their steps from the night before. It gave the grass a cream-like patina. This time she had dressed for the cold, wearing Cora's canvas barn coat. She hadn't thought to bring warm clothes from California and the coat, while baggy for Cora, was too small for to her button. She leaned the steel rake against her shoulder, its teeth pointing behind her back as she headed across the front lawn to the farm road. She hadn't paid that much attention to the farm buildings since her arrival, but after Uncle Jack's comments at the cemetery she turned at the edge of the road and looked back. The house, the shed, and the barn were physically connected, of one piece. The house and shed looked down the road, while the large barn jutted out from end of the shed at a right angle, it's huge open door like a monstrous mouth facing her. Everything under the same roof, she realized, the people and the animals, their food and water, the firewood and the hay.

She stopped again at the cemetery, stood inside the white birches that encircled it. The early morning sun glistened off their golden leaves and the frost on the long grass beside the gravestones. She counted 12 graves in three rows, two rows of five, one of two. She walked each row reading the names, some barely decipherable, worn by the weather and encrusted with lichen—Isaiah Irish, Jonah Irish, Theophilus Cooper, Rebecca Lowell, Elwood Cooper, Emily Gordon, Angela Lowell, Amelia Petty. The dates on the stones that could be read ranged from 1873 to 1951.

Completing the tour, she walked back to the grave of Angela Lowell. She thought it a curious and unwelcome coincidence that of only 12 gravestones, one should bear her first name. The dates declared a short life for this Angela: 1910–1916. She had never given much thought to her name, that it could have any significance, or to her life ever ending, for that matter. Something rustled through the trees beyond, waking her to her appointed task. She stepped backwards through the birch trees staring into the cemetery as she returned to the farm road.

The task at the spring was underwhelming. With five strokes of the rake across the top of the water, the leaves bunched at the pool's edge, forming a lumpy curb. She swung the steel tines into it, flinging the wet wads away. Leaves also lay like a thick rug on the ground next to the spring and Angela cleared a three-foot ring around the pool. She realized there were many still to fall from the surrounding trees and noted the possibility that Uncle Jack might add this to her chores over the coming days.

***

Aunt Cora looked up from her morning coffee at Angela's return, still in her light-blue bathrobe and slippers, her gray hair flat against her head. "That wasn't too hard, was it dear?" she asked.

"Pretty easy, actually," Angela returned. "Still a lot of leaves to fall. I'll probably have to go back."

117

" 'Least it's a pretty walk up there this time of year. Hear any shots fired? Hunting season just started, you might want to wear some bright colors and not my brown barn coat."

"I'm sorry, I should have asked if I could wear it."

"No problem, Dear. Your uncle's orange cap is out in the shed some place. You can wear that too."

Angela poured herself a coffee and joined her aunt at the table. "What can you tell me about the cemetery up the road, about those people?" She asked.

Aunt Cora was slow to answer, the question hanging in the space between them. She appeared to be looking out the kitchen window for the answer. "Not much, you should talk to your uncle. He's the house authority on that subject."

"There's a child buried there. Her name was Angela Lowell. Six years old when she died. I can't believe there's somebody with my name in that little cemetery. Weird, don't you think?"

Cora continued to stare out the window at the maple tree, its brilliant red leaves waving in a slight wind. "You should probably get ready for work, don't you think." It was not a question.

***

Angela arrived early for her noon-to-eight shift at the True Value. She wondered what lay behind Aunt Cora's curious reaction to her question and was anxious to talk to Uncle Jack about the cemetery. She hoped they could steal some free time together during the usual mid-afternoon customer lull. But when she approached him about it, he told her it would have to wait until she got home that night. It was not something to discuss at the store. Some kind of mystery, she supposed, and could barely concentrate on her work for the rest of the day, speculating on what it might be.

***

"Want the long version or the short?" Jack asked, as the uncle and niece sat down in the living room, fledgling flames lighting up the fireplace sending a soft warmth into the air. "What do you want to know?" His large hands clutched the arms of the rocking chair.

Angela, tired from her long day, sat at the edge of the sofa, her small frame straight, her soft features tightened in anticipation. "About the cemetery, why is it even there? What do you know about those people?" She struggled to find a word. "Reverence, when you showed me the graves last night and talked to them or about them—the people, not the graves—there was a reverence to it. Is that the word I want?"

"Maybe, I don't know reverence from reference," he said through a broad smile, emphasizing the "v" and "f" sounds. "Let's begin with the farm. We'd heard about it in California from some friends in Maine, but it took a while to find it. It dates back to the mid-nineteenth century, 1850 or there-abouts. When we bought it in 1975, it had been empty for twenty years. We got it for $10,000 from Bud Kimball, a local farmer who only used it for the hay fields every year. Never lived in it. He had bought it in the '60's for next to nothing. Imagine, only $10,000 for these buildings and fifty acres of land. No phone. Never been wired for electric. The closest pole a half mile away. The plumbing gravity-fed, like I explained last night. Served the kitchen sink, a sink and a bathtub in the bathroom, and the water barrel in the barn. Cold water. No toilet, outhouse in the shed, as you know. Wasn't insulated. Cook stove was a Queen Atlantic, half wood, half bottled gas. Another wood stove in the dining area and a fireplace in the living room to heat the house. Two ice boxes. One, a real one we used for a cupboard and one that operated on propane gas. Imagine that, a gas flame that heats water and ammonia that reacts with hydrogen gas to create cold. Counter intuitive, I'd say." He paused to catch his breath.

"Imagine this place, sitting at the end of a half mile of dirt

119

road on a high piece of land all by its lonesome, surrounded by ten acres of field, forty of wood lot, a diamond in the rough, a real find and a hell of a project. For the first three years we lived in the kitchen while we brought the place into the twentieth century. Our bed was where the kitchen table is now. Did I say we own those power poles that come up the road to the house? Put them in myself."

Jack took another deep breath. "Are you still with me?"

"Oh yes," Angela replied.

"I'm telling you all this so you get a picture of how the people lying in those graves lived. A life of hard work just to stay warm and fed even during a time when most everyone else in the state was enjoying electricity, oil furnaces, and phones. Which brings me to who they were - the people that built this house and worked this land for a hundred years or so were Shakers."

Angela laughed. "What do you mean? Like they were nervous or had Parkinson's?"

Jack smiled at her reaction. "No. Heaven forbid. The Shakers were, and still are, a religious sect. The United Society of Believers in Christ's Second Appearing is their formal name. They're called Shakers because their bodies shake when they experience intense religious moments, revelations, out-of body-experiences, I guess you could call 'em."

Jack looked into the fire. "But that's not what's important for me," he continued, his words slowing. "It's how they live their lives, simply, no frills, make the best use of God's gifts, grow their own food, weave their own cloth, are as independent as possible, understand and rely on the natural world, are in sync with it." He paused to take a deep breath.

"They're pacifists, you know. And they believe men and women are equal in all respects, believe in equality for all people in this country of racial and social divide." He looked toward Angela. "What is odd about the cemetery is the grave of that child, Angela Lowell."

"Why is that odd?" Angela asked, surprised that Jack had

landed on the question, the topic she wanted the most. And he had brought it up before she did.

"Because there are few, if any children, in Shaker communities because they don't believe in marriage or sex." Jack paused, a little embarrassed now by this turn the conversation was taking with the niece he barely knew.

"That's crazy. Why not?" Angela asked, her curiosity heightened.

Jack looked into the fire again, taking a moment to collect his thoughts. "In the seventeen and eighteen hundred's, and even into this century, a marriage was like a legal contract, giving the husband control over his wife, maybe not so stated but definitely implied. It meant a loss of freedom for a wife, even the freedom for her to refuse intercourse with her husband."

"That can't be right!"

"That's what the Shakers say. They believe that Jesus is the symbolic male version of God and their founder, Mother Ann, is the female version. They believe that God is equally alive in both men and women, and as Jesus was not married and a virgin, so women must be as well. They expect their followers to live these beliefs, no marriage or sex, to ensure those truths in their lives. In fact, they are even known for giving refuge to women escaping from abusive husbands. You have to realize this was well before there were any social services for battered women or laws against domestic abuse.

***

"Angela suddenly felt disoriented as a of wave anxiety swept over her. The room blurred; her uncle's form grew distant. Images of her ex-boyfriend appeared, memories of violent moments she had repressed: the brutal, choking grasp of his hands around her throat, the sharp sting and screech of fabric ripped from her body, the slaps on her buttocks, at first playful, then painful. So sudden and unexpected, triggered by any disagreement, however reasonable. Then the overwhelming fear of rejecting him, of breaking it off, of what he would do if she did.

Tears overwhelmed her sight as she sobbed and turned her head away from her uncle, who slowly rose from his chair and sat beside her on the couch, gently putting his arm around her shoulder. "You don't have to say anything, Angie," he said. "We know why you're here. And we're here for you." He wanted so to comfort her, but at this critical moment was at a loss for words. Was this the time to tell her? Of course it was. "And you know, that girl with your name in the cemetery, I think that's why she is here. Her mother arrived without a husband but with a child. What would drive her into the arms of the Shakers? Why would they welcome her? Why would the child die so young? I've thought about this. There was no way she could ever be found here with them."

Calamity

Calamity Joe and Calam
ity Jane form a rock band,
"Restless Hobos,"
Jane on oboe,
Joe on the spoons and the fry pan.

Calamity Jane and Calam
ity Joe buy a Vanagon
To hit the spots,
The parking lots,
To follow the Stones and their fans.

Calamity Joe and Calam
ity Jane, their gear well in hand,
Busk the grills,
The tail gate stills,
The oboe's voice their special brand.

Calamity Jane and Calam
ity Joe, whirling in a dance,
Franticly freed
By the oboe's reeds
And the beat from the spoons and pan.

Calamity Joe's and Calam
ity Jane's syncopated jazz:
From head to toe
The rhythm throws
The cares of the world off their backs

Calamity Jane and Calam
ity Joe say that that's the plan:
The weird and wild
Distract the eye
From the worries and pain at hand.

Calamity Joe and Calam
Ity Jane's very funky jam
Catches his ear
As Jagger nears,
Feet dancing the pan's commands.

Who would have thought a frying pan
And oboe could excite this man
Of world-wide fame
And great acclaim
To move with such abandon.

Calamity Jane and Calamity Joe

It wasn't until she broke her foot that Jane took up the oboe. Nearly immobile in the ugly black boot, she found little to occupy her time or teenage energy. Television bored her, reading had always been a struggle and, as the only child to busy parents either working or otherwise engaged, boredom finally got the best of her. A shy, thin 14-year-old with few friends, she painfully missed her long jogs around the park across from her home, unknowingly addicted to the feel-good endorphins that blessed her daily ritual.

The oboe certainly wouldn't have been her first choice. It had been almost thrust upon her by the music teacher in this first month of her freshman year at Orion High School, the result of a circuitous set of circumstances. The first was the opinion paper assigned in English class asking for three paragraphs on *"What Bores Me the Most—what it is, why it is, what to do about it."* Jane chose the rap and hip-hop music her contemporaries listened to almost constantly. As she explained in her paper, she had grown up with the classical music her mother enjoyed while making dinner and the Chet Atkins, Miles Davis and Kenny G that rode with her and her dad to school each day. There was something intensely provocative about both, she explained, that lifted her out of reality, whereas rap, on the other hand, was mired in it. She had gotten an "A", with the comment "Well done."

***

The music teacher stopped her in the hall. A tall, willowy woman with an intense presence, Ms. Emery approached Jane with flattery and a proposition. Mr. Sebastian had told her about Jane's excellent paper, the school orchestra needed an oboe, and Jane's description of the music she loved was the oboe's home. Would Jane consider learning and playing the oboe in the school orchestra?

"I know this sounds crazy. I'm just asking that you think about it," Ms. Emery said. "We have the instrument, so you won't have to buy it, and I can give you lessons, at least to get started. I'm free period five and after school each day. From what Mr. Sebastian said, you might find you have an affinity for the oboe and not even know it."

The proposition was ridiculous. It was as if an alien being had entered her world and momentarily altered her reality. She had never considered playing a musical instrument, let alone one as weird as an oboe. She shook off the thought as she headed to class.

Then Jane broke her foot at the homecoming dance, dancing by herself on the bottom bleacher in the darkened gym, losing her balance, falling awkwardly on her ankle. She was to stay off it as much as possible, wear the boot, use the crutches if necessary, but still go to school. It would take at least six weeks to heal if she was a good girl, the doctor said. Much longer if she ignored him.

"Don't get fooled when the pain subsides and you think you can dance again," he said. "Be a patient patient, and you'll be back on the dance floor before you know it."

***

By the second week of immobility she was dispirited and impatient. She needed a distraction from the routines of school and home, being housebound on weekends, too much television, too little face-to-face peer interaction, and no rejuvenating run. Riding to school with her dad one day, she let

126

his morning music embrace her.

"What are we listening to, Dad?" she asked. "*Witchi Tai To*," he said. "The Paul Winter Consort. That's Paul McCandles, on the oboe. It's what makes the song so evocative. Cool, isn't it? Both Native American and jazz. Not something you'd necessarily associate with jazz. Jim Pepper has a rendition of this as well, but I think McCandless really takes this to another level."

Jane didn't respond. Her head went immediately back to the music. The oboe's haunting solo took her to a place far away from her unhappy circumstances. They were approaching the school entrance and she didn't want the moment to end. As the car came to the curb, she barely heard her dad through the music.

"Here we are, Kiddo, have a nice day," he said.

Limping toward the school, she noticed Ms. Emery ahead of her. She felt an unexpected impulse to catch up, but that was impossible. She decided if she happened to see her again, within hobbling distance, she might reconsider the teacher's proposition.

***

In the fall of Jane's senior year, while taking her seat in the orchestra's wind section, Jane was distracted by Joe Drago as he walked past her. Oddly she had never really noticed him before, even though he had been just a few rows behind her for the previous three years. It was his blonde hair, most of it standing up straight, and his jaunty stride that caught her eye as he passed by to get to the timpani section. Or maybe it was the square, solid build under the red and green plaid shirt and the shy smile she thought was directed at her. She turned her head to let her eyes follow him. He was standing at the snare, sticks in hand, looking directly at her. Jane, slightly embarrassed, immediately turned back to her music.

***

Joe approached her after Ms. Emery dismissed the class, sitting himself down on the folding chair beside her. "Hi, what class do you have next?" he asked.

"Physics," she replied, slowly putting her instrument back in its case so as to not to look at him.

"Well, it's a bit out of my way, but maybe I could walk you there?"

The question caught her by surprise. Two options were available, only one of which required an explanation which she didn't have. Turning to face him, showing a hesitant smile and getting to her feet, she said, "Sure. We should get going."

On the cusp of 18 years old, Jane was now a striking young woman with long, curly black hair that seemed to defy gravity, high cheek bones, and luminous blue eyes. Easily six feet tall, her presence was impossible to ignore. Joe Drago felt uncomfortably short walking beside her and a bit intimidated, but was not deterred from his mission.

"I'm really impressed by your playing," he began, "really impressed." He would have liked to tell her how attractive he found her but didn't have the courage or the words for that. "I want to start a band," he began. "A rock band that features an oboe. You know, like Jethro Tull and Traffic and Peter Gabriel feature the flute. What really got me thinking about this was drumming along with B'ela Fleck and the Flecktones at home the other night. 'Sinister Minister.' You should hear it sometime. There's an oboe part that's so cool. You play really well. Do you sing?"

Unable to absorb what she'd heard, Jane wanted him to start over. "What are you talking about? What kind of band?"

"A band, you know, like the ones I mentioned, only with an oboe instead of a flute. Just you and me."

"Just the two of us? You're crazy." She stopped abruptly. "Here's my class." She pointed to the door ahead. "And there's my locker across the hall. I've got to get my books. See you in orchestra." Jane quickly turned and walked across a trail of students, leaving Joe behind. He'd be late to his next class but didn't care. *Mission accomplished*, he said to himself as he watched her disappear into physics.

Jane couldn't concentrate during the presentation on quantum mechanics. Didn't take a single note. It wasn't so much Joe's proposition that occupied her thoughts, as it was his compliments about her oboe, the instrument she'd learned to love. She'd found it difficult to play at first, the double reed a challenge. But once she had agreed, she had fully accepted Ms. Emery's challenge and fought the frustrations. It was the first real commitment she had made to an adult other than her parents and she didn't want to let her down. Jane remembered how the first rare pure tones she produced had excited her with an overwhelming visceral sensation. And how the joy that accompanied overcoming each of the oboe's challenges empowered her to meet the next. Joe's idea was absurd, she concluded, and she turned her attention as best she could to the physics lesson.

***

Joe was not crazy. A bit obsessed with this one idea, but otherwise a normal high school senior. He was still considering his options after graduation. College didn't interest him, at least not right away. Maybe he'd study to be architect. He had a gift for drawing. But he wanted a year off. His obsession these last few months was to form a band, an acoustic band, something simple and clean and unique, not messy and loud and full of itself. He would visualize the options - his drums with a fiddle or sax or acoustic guitar. He imagined how he could pare down his drum set to just a snare or tambourine, or even a wash board. Lately he had been experimenting with a frying pan.

There was a mental picture that kept recurring of him

beside the beautiful Jane, playing her oboe, while he accompanied her with rhythmic riffs. *An unrealistic aspiration?* he asked himself. Perhaps, but not if he committed to it. He knew it was unusual, would take some convincing, and that the odds were slim. "Nothing ventured, nothing gained," his mom always said. He would put on the full-court press. He had nothing to lose.

***

When Jane entered her next orchestra class, Joe was sitting in her seat. She wanted to avoid him but didn't see how. Joe had rehearsed his plea. He would repeat his praise of her prowess, extol the advantage of playing only music she enjoyed, and magnify the fun they would have doing their own thing. He'd propose no commitment, just a trial session to see if it would work.

"Excuse me," Jane said standing at the end of her row. "You're in my seat."

Joe stood up and moved to the seat to his left as Jane moved down the row to sit beside him. As she opened her oboe's case, Joe began. "I want you to know how much I enjoy hearing you play. You're really good."

Jane immediately cut him off. "Not now, not here," she said, her words clipped with authority. "Can you meet me after school tomorrow in the cafeteria? We can talk then."

"Yeah, I can do that," Joe answered without hesitation, surprised that Jane had so abruptly taken control.

"You'd better get to your drums," she said, sending him away.

As much as she didn't want to admit it, Jane was intrigued by his idea. It being so unexpected it reminded her of Ms. Emery's proposal her freshman year and how finally mastering the oboe had been so rewarding. After exhausting Ms. Emery's knowledge, she had taken lessons after school from an oboist who lived a few blocks away. With little to do

130

for over a month but her homework and practicing the instrument, she was surprised by her progress and how much fun it was to play. She enjoyed exploring the range of sounds from rich and robust to bright and keen. Sometimes she took advantage of her dad's vinyl and CD collection, attempting to imitate the embedded solos of the best oboists. Over that first year she discovered she could play by ear and found herself often ignoring the sheet music after a first reading, much to Ms. Emery's displeasure.

Jane, very much an introvert, now found herself as intrigued about making music with Joe as she was fearful of embarrassing herself with him. She had been looking for something to move her beyond the day-to-day. This could be it. She needed to know more about what he had in mind. But she struggled to picture a "band" of just an oboe and a drum, of just him and her.

***

The cafeteria seemed larger than usual with most of the tables stacked against the walls. Two remained set up near the entrance and Jane chose a seat so she could see Joe when he entered the room. She wanted him to sit across from her, not beside her.

He appeared suddenly with the same animated walk, a broad smile above his square jaw, one hand behind his back. He was headed for her side of the table and she stood up and gestured to the seat across from hers. He changed course, finally standing where she had directed him. "Have a seat," she said, as if this was her office and she was greeting a client. Before he sat down, however, Joe brought a green metal frying pan out from behind his back, setting it on the table. He then pulled the tail of his red plaid shirt out of his belt along with a drum stick that had been hiding behind it and sat down. "There," he said, his smile widening. "That was pretty uncomfortable. Brought these for show and tell."

131

"What?" Jane asked, still standing. "Show and tell?"

"Exactly, that's exactly why I brought them. You probably thought you'd be playing the oboe while I sat hammering away behind a drum set. How boring would that be? Pretty boring, don't you think? It would be like those groups that play at the museum."

Jane didn't know what he was talking about.

"I hate these bands where they all just stand in one place and the singer roams around the stage or runs around it, staring down into the crowd. It's like they're trying to make a connection but keeping a safe distance. They're up there on the stage but the crowd's down below. Where's the connection in that? I want to show you something."

Joe stood up, grabbing the fry pan and drum stick as he stood. Walking into the empty cafeteria space he beat out a rhythm on the pan, accentuating different tones when he hit the pan's bottom, side, rim, and surface. Even the pan's handle. He held the drumstick between his fingers at the middle of its shaft, using both its tip and butt, alternately hitting the pan's rim and surface.

Joe began to dance to the rhythms from the pan, his sneakers lifting him off his feet, the pan slapping his thigh for cadence between differing tempos. His loose shirt flew behind him as he spun across the floor. Then, stopping abruptly, his footwork accelerated, still commanded by the pan.

Jane was mesmerized and confused by what she saw. He seemed out of control. What was he listening to in his head to construct this? Was he under the influence of something other than inspiration? What was the point, she wondered, forgetting why she was there.

***

He stopped in the middle of the cafeteria floor. Out of breath, he took a moment to collect himself. "Pretty crazy,

132

don't you think?" he said, smiling, walking toward Jane. "I've
been working on this for over a month, gettin' the hang of it
all. I'm experimenting with long-handle spoons too, instead
of sticks."

Joe stopped to take a breath.

"What if a band was in the middle of the people, on the
same level, like its one of them, without the amps and the
speakers and wires and mics?" he continued. "What if the
band danced with the audience, weaving among them? Kind
of like the pied piper, but not going anywhere. You know, just
hanging around, getting 'em going, setting an example."

Jane had gotten to her feet and Joe was now at the table
standing across from her. "Next time bring your oboe. We can
try this together. You play some dancing music and I'll
accompany you."

"Next time?" Jane asked, at a loss for words, their meeting ending so abruptly.

"Yeah, next time. How about next Monday, give you time
to come up with something danceable, if that's a word, and
you join me on the oboe. Just let me know what it is before
hand. Monday, same time, same place. Does that work?"

"I guess," she said. Joe gave her a thumbs up and walked
out of the cafeteria, swinging the frying pan to match his
stride.

***

On her way home Jane replayed the vision of Joe's dance
as she considered his proposal. Crazy as it was, it looked like
great fun, his exuberance and joy overwhelming her hesitancy. Could she do this? she wondered. Let herself go like that?
So out of character. He had asked her twice now if she could
sing. Did he expect that? Not in her comfort zone and out of
the question. Jane knew she could immerse herself in her
oboe, close her eyes, hide behind their lids and let the music
flow from her fingers. She had made no commitment. There

133

was time to think it over.

In order to choose a song with enough pizzazz to arouse Joe's dance, she thought of her dad's music and that seminal moment riding to school and hearing the oboe solo that had so captivated her. Jane had not heard it since that day. By necessity she had concentrated on the music for orchestra. She could only remember the context, its spirit and feel. She also remembered Joe mentioning a song she should listen to, which she had also forgotten. She would not embarrass herself by asking him. She was equally certain that her dad would never remember what they were listening to that morning. What she did remember was its Native American feel. Maybe that would help.

She found him in the kitchen drying the dishes. "Hey, Dad, I'm wondering if you remember some Native American jazz you might have been listening to a few years ago that featured an oboe? I remember one I really liked we listened to on one of our rides to school freshman year, but can't remember what it was. "

"Sure, let's see," he replied. "Maybe Jim Pepper? No, that's saxophone. There's Carlos Nakai, but he plays flute. Great stuff. The Paul Winter Consort, maybe 'Witchi Tai-To.' There's a great oboe solo in that song. Does that help?"

"I think that's it. Do you still have the cd?"

"Of course. I'll get it for you when I finish the dishes."

Listening to it again, she relived the experience in the car. They might have to increase the tempo to meet Joe's wishes, but it seemed perfect. She sent an MP3 to Joe. She added a note: *If I'm playing, you'll have to sing.*

"Perfect" was Joe's response.

***

When they met in the cafeteria the next Monday afternoon, Joe sang the song a capella with a heightened tempo, before adding a complimentary beat from the frying pan.

Then, with a combination of hits and strokes and his perfect-pitch tenor, the song engulfed the large room as Joe weaved and bobbed. Completing the second verse, he nodded to Jane to play the oboe solo she had practiced all week. Joe danced around her, his body swinging from side to side, lifting his legs with his knees as he imitated Native American dance.

It was magical for both of them. After the oboe's solo, Jane found herself singing along. her voice a soft, beautiful shadow to Joe's, the perfect compliment.

Two students who had watched unnoticed from the doorway applauded. Joe bowed in their direction. Jane blushed. It was a moment of truth for both of them—Joe realizing his dream and Jane overcoming her fear. Where it would lead remained uncertain, but the adrenalin that exploded for both begged for an encore. They agreed to meet again, same place, same time, same assignments.

***

Eight months later they ended a Monday session with their repertoire of nine well-rehearsed songs and a declaration of purpose. They had forged a relationship threaded with musical trials, uncertainty, awkward moments, shared joy, questioned ambition, and an anxious anticipation to show off their stuff. It was early May and the spring sun cast shadows of budding trees on the cafeteria floor. They had finished practicing their rendition of "Psycho Killer" and, with the last note, bowed to each other and embraced. The school year was ending, graduation loomed. As did summer, a preparatory prequel to college for Jane, an empty field for Joe to grow his dream. This was it. They were ready. The Walmart parking lot on Saturday. The vast section near the McDonalds that was rarely occupied. The weather report promised a beautiful day, full sun, high '60s.

"Are you nervous?" Joe asked Jane.

"What do you think, of course, aren't you?"

"A little. You're not gonna back out, are you? After all this?"

Jane smiled her commitment to their effort. "I never imagined I would spend a year doing this."

"I imagined it,"Joe replied, "but didn't believe it would happen. You're really something else."

Jane blushed. "I'll take that as a compliment. What time are you picking me up?

"Noon. Have you told your parents?"

"No, not yet. Have you?"

"Not gonna."

"I think I might," Jane replied. "I mean, I want to tell them, but I don't want them to come. I know they'll want to, but I don't know how they'll react. They've been so cool about this all year. And by cool I don't mean supportive. I mean sort of blasé. I think they never thought it would amount to anything. I think I gave them that impression. Now I'm not sure what to do."

"I get it. That's why I'm not telling mine. I want to have at least one real busk, one full dress rehearsal in front of an audience before they see us." Neither admitted the nagging fear of cold feet or failure. He lifted his arm up around her shoulders as they walked out into the cool spring sunlight. They had become close friends, and the impending event promised to be the ultimate bonding experience.

***

Driving into the Walmart parking lot, they found a scattering of cars. Joe drove to the largest empty area, parked, and took a deep breath. Without speaking they stepped into the sunlight, Jane with her oboe, Joe with his spoons and frying pan, wearing a harmonica bracketed to his neck. There would be no amplification. The music would have to lift above the scuffle and swoosh of a busy town. They had not anticipated this. No matter, there was no turning back.

"Ready?" Joe asked. Jane responded with a quick run up a scale on her oboe and the first notes of "Day Tripper." Joe bobbed his head as she played the repeating 13-note refrain, then banged the underlying beat on the frying pan's bottom.

"Got a good reason,
For taking the easy way out.
Yeah, got a good reason
For taking the easy way out."

They sang together, replicating the song's close harmony as Joe hit the driving beat. Jane, a head taller than Joe, her black curls catching the sun, swayed with the music as Joe enlarged the arc of his dance. Curious shoppers stopped briefly to listen, only to continue on to their cars.

Joe suddenly stopped and waved the frying pan at Jane. "They're walking away. We've got to get closer to the store, closer to the door," he said, sounding frantic. "Come on, follow me!" He hurriedly led her to a rare empty parking space at the edge of the crosswalk to the front door. "Let's do 'Witchi Tai-To.' "

While he tightened the screws on his harmonica holder, Joe wailed a blues riff into the air, then jogged closer to the cross-walk as he began the song. With an up-tempo beat on the frying pan, his body leaning forward, the harmonica swinging like a rough, heavy necklace, his knees rose and fell to stomp quick dance steps. Joe danced across the crosswalk. Jane hesitantly followed.

In front of Walmart's front door Joe circled the sidewalk, then led Jane back across the crosswalk to the parking lane. Shoppers, gathering around them, followed - a captive audience that grew with every measure of the song. It was everything Joe had dreamed of. They were pied pipers capturing the imagination of the onlookers with their music.

With the song's ending they immediately launched into "Psycho Killer." Immersed in their music, then didn't hear the sirens heralding the approach of the police. It was only when the officer pushed through the crowd to face Jane that the music stopped.

"Stop," he ordered, his voice loud with authority. "There's been a complaint. You're disturbing the peace. What exactly is going on here?"

Stunned, Jane was speechless and immediately turned to look for Joe. Where was he? He could explain. This was his idea, not hers.

"Look at me," the officer demanded, aggravated that she was not responding. "What are you doing here? This is dangerous. You need permission for something like this. Come with me, please." He grabbed her upper arm to lead her toward his cruiser. "Where's the other one? I was told there were two of you?"

Jane turned her head back toward the crowd, thinking Joe had followed them. The officer's grip tightened as she resisted. Joe was not there. He should have been by her side by now. He should be by her side.

"He's behind me," she answered, her voice ragged.

"Over there, we're going over there to my cruiser. Do you see it? I don't want to drag you. I want you to walk by my side. Can I trust you'll do that? Nothing's gonna happen. You're not under arrest or anything like that. I just need to get your information. Okay? Can I let go?"

"Yes, please." Jane was crying now, her face flushed. Reaching the cruiser, she scanned the parking lot. The car was gone. Joe's car was gone.

Indecision

Indecision doesn't flow.
It's meter falters as it goes
Toward a choice,
A jagged voice,
A back and forth staccato.

What lies behind that closed door?
Shouldn't we explore this more?
Or take a step,
Just move ahead
In spite of what we wanted more?

Notwithstanding this or that,
Surely we must hold fast,
But then, again,
One more question,
"Is there more to this?" you ask.

Adirondack Snowe

Exercising her pandemic vigilance, Adirondack Snowe sensed there was a car at the foot of her long, steep driveway, at the bottom of the gravel incline that led to her modest home high among the trees. A faint crunch of tires on crushed stone alerted her to its presence. Moving to the window, her binoculars in hand, a wave of anxiety surged across her forehead in anticipation of the potential viral invasion. She had not left the house in days, relying on her well-stocked cupboards and freezer for the essentials. She had never been a hoarder until the deadly virus swept through the state, from the coast, up the river, into the mountains behind Lake Tear of the Clouds. Approaching the window, she slowed, listening for the car's advance or retreat to the main road, hoping for the latter.

It was still there. She watched the driver emerge. A man in a denim jacket and baseball cap looked up to her house and began his ascent, his head down, his stride long and determined. He was not wearing a mask. It was her worst fear. Was he lost? Did he want directions? Did he need to use the phone? Was it car trouble? Why here, why not at the gas station he had passed a mile back?

Or maybe it was Publisher's Clearing House with the first installment of $5,000 a week for the rest of her life? The thought made her smile and leveled her rising anxiety as he drew closer. She lowered the binoculars. He was quite tall and lean and wore those snug blue jeans that were rarely

140

seen in the mountains. A sling bag hung off his right shoulder, swinging slightly with each step, his head down as he concentrated on the climb. *Maybe thirty, no more than thirty-five*, she estimated.

Adirondack rarely walked the hill now; her arthritis was unforgiving. She even found it difficult to work in the garden that sat on a quarter acre of level ground behind the house, a rare dent in the slope of the mountain. After just a few minutes of her much-loved pastime, with all the bending and crouching, the pain in her knees would assert its dominance.

As he neared the stairs to the front porch, she brushed the few stray gray hairs off her shoulders and straightened her light green house dress, her brown eyes intensely focused on the visitor. As usual, she was not prepared for company and suddenly felt self-conscious. She decided to anticipate his knock and surprise him with an open door, leaving only the locked storm door between them. "Hello," he said as he topped the porch stairs and saw her though the glass.

"Yes?" The word as a question, a slight anxious tension in her voice.

"Are you Adirondack Snowe?" He pushed his cap up off his narrow face. "Love the name, by the way." He was wearing a white shirt and tie, mostly hidden behind a black sweater and worn denim jacket.

"Yes."

"Rio, Dr. Rio Watson," he said, extending his right hand toward the glass door as if to shake hers through it.

"The door's locked. They call me Addy. What do you want?" Her eyes focused behind him back to the car at the bottom of the drive, afraid he was not alone, that there were others, that this was how home invaders operated, masquerading as a single visitor only to suddenly multiply and overwhelm.

"I didn't see a number on your mailbox. This is 85 Iroquois Road, right?"

"Yes, what to do you want?"

"I'm a professor at Syracuse University, archaeological science. I would have called but couldn't find your number. I sent a couple letters, but never heard back. We believe there could be an ancient Native American site on your property, a significant one, perhaps dating back to 7,000 B.C. My students have been researching this general area for a year now. With aerial thermal imaging we've been able to search for sites unobtrusively, with drones and such."

Too much information, too much talk for Addy. "What do you want? Make it brief please. You're not wearing a mask. I can't let you in with the pandemic and all."

"I'm sorry," Rio responded. "To be brief, we'd like your permission to investigate a site on your property, behind your house, do a small dig, nothing intrusive. I've brought the paperwork with me, I could leave it with you. We would do no harm, leave everything the way we found it."

"A dig for what?"

"Bone harpoons, arrow heads. We have some evidence that a long house sat on your property potentially leaving many artifacts. It sat close to that abrupt elevation rise behind your house. We believe that the odd flattening of the land here on the mountain side was at least partially the work of man."

Addy, accustomed to a predictable daily routine, governed by her, with few decisions of any kind, was out of her element. Dealing with the out-of-nowhere was frightening. This didn't make sense, this guy in jeans and a tie, a shoulder bag and Yankees cap. "I can't do this," she simultaneously thought and said.

"Can you please at least think about it?" Rio pleaded. "My students were so excited to find this site, have so hoped to explore it, to dig. There is rich history here to uncover. You could even help. It can be very exciting to unearth artifacts, enter an earlier age, to learn this way. I will leave the paperwork with you. My card is attached. Please call me one way or the other. This may be a bad time with the pandemic and all, but we will be outside, there would be no need to make close contact with us." Rio lay the paperwork on the porch in front of the storm door. "We were hoping to begin mid-spring. Have a good day, Ms. Snowe."

Addy watched him return to his car, then looked back into the house as if an answer were there. She was suddenly conflicted, her instinctual reaction tempered by a sympathy for his research and for the students awaiting his return. A teacher by trade, spinster by choice, and a recluse by temperament, she had retired after 40 years of lovable first graders filling an otherwise empty space in her heart. Her very few friends were fellow teachers, a younger, vibrant professional family that shared the joy and challenges of the classroom. Now they were busy teaching and she was not.

She had struggled to settle herself that first September at home when she wanted to be meeting her new students and embracing their innocent, lively enthusiasm. Now, her retirement and the pandemic challenged her proclivity for isolation. Often she would rationalize that she might be alone but not lonesome. But there were moments when the absence of a helping hand or a friend's support disturbed her emotional equilibrium.

She was convinced her name was at the root of her insecurities and never forgave her parents, growing up uncomfortable with it, wanting to disown it. She had been conceived on her parents' honeymoon in a hotel in Lake Placid during a snowstorm. "A lot of people hate their name," her father used to say. "Get over it. Just use the nickname. Everybody calls you 'Addy.' And, by the way, Adirondack works so well with your last name, don't you think?"

***

She let the contract sit face-up on the kitchen island for two days. She needed to think through the pros and cons of

Rio's request, her privacy pitted against his students' hands-on learning that was so successful with her own students. His plea was vividly recalled, his assertion of its significance in his soft-spoken, polite manner. And the name Rio, unusual, maybe as unforgiving as hers. Why Rio? Was there a similar story behind it that gave it a significance he could not escape, that altered his life as she was convinced her's had?

Watching television, reading a book, making dinner, cleaning the house, her attention would abruptly drift to the dilemma that consumed her. After four days she decided to decide, poured herself two fingers of scotch, walked into the back-yard, and stared into the trees behind the garden, imagining as best she could the possible lives Rio suggested had come before. For years she had explored the woods, beckoned into them by their rustle in soft breezes, often surprised to find a patch of day-lilies or a stray lilac, even a few strawberry plants, hugging the bases of trees at the edge of small clearings. Maybe these were not an accident of nature. Maybe they had been planted there, surviving many millennia to bear witness. The thought comforted her. Notwithstanding her reservations, she would call Rio and let him know that she wanted him to find out.

***

It was late April when Rio and his 12 students arrived to begin the dig, staying in off- season rentals in Spectacular, arriving early in the morning and working until dark, Friday through Sunday. They set up a small canopy on her back lawn and concentrated their search along the edge of the tree line. From the moment they arrived, they seemed to know exactly where to look.

The pandemic was easing, but Addy remained hypercautious, distancing herself from the students as she sat watching on the steps to the back door, excited to have such novelty in her life. She had declined Rio's offer to let her help, not wanting to get too close or in the way. It was enough just to have this curious distraction disrupting the usual monotony of her life.

Late in the afternoon on a Saturday three weeks into their efforts, Rio knocked on the back door. Addy was slow to respond, wiping her hands of the residue of the pizza dough from the treat she was preparing for the students. They were her students now. Just watching and listening to them she learned their names, noting their distinguishing characteristics, and smiling at their busy banter. These weekends had become an unexpected joy and she wanted to give back. What better way than pizza and beer at the end of their long day.

Rio's insistent knock suddenly got her full attention. "What is it?" she called out. "I'll be right there."

"We've found something. We need to talk," Rio answered.

"Okay, great," Addy replied, surprised by her own excitement for his.

"Can I come in, please? I don't want to do this outside," she heard him say as she approached the door.

"Where's your mask?" she asked.

"In the van."

"You get yours, I'll get mine." For Rio, this meant running down the hill to the van and climbing back up to the house. *Give me a break*, he thought as he closed the door behind him.

***

"What we found is not what we are here for," Rio began, keeping his distance, standing across the kitchen island from her, catching his breath. "It is on the work table under the canopy. You need to take a look. Being on your property, they belong to you. Just out of curiosity, how long have you lived here?"

"I don't know. Like forever, thirty years, give or take.

145

Why? I bought it in '85, at least I think it was '85, maybe '86".

"Let's go out side. We'll keep our distance."

The students circled the perimeter of the canopied work space as Rio and Addy entered. On the table sat three greenish, rusted metal containers, identical, the shape and size of small shoe boxes, each clasped with a small steel padlock. "I thought about prying them open at first, curious, you know, without thinking," Rio began to explain. "You get into a mindset when digging like this. You get excited about any little thing that might justify the effort, so the first thought is always, you know, what have I found? What have I discovered? As if it's yours. Then you step back and realize that none of it's really yours. An historic artifact is everybody's, except in this case, these are not historic or artifacts, Addy. This is your property we're on. What's on it and below it is yours. I was just going to bring them to you without all this fanfare, but my guys and gals found them, and wanted to be here for the handover. They're very curious, as you might guess. Do these things mean anything to you?"

Addy looked at the metal containers, then to the students at the edges, and then to Rio. "No, no they don't. I don't know what to say," she replied. It was not what she had expected and she suddenly felt the familiar anxiety that accompanied the unpredictable. "Can you tell how long they've been buried there? Did you find any keys with them? How would I open them?"

"The hinges are quite rusted. Most likely you could wedge them open with a screwdriver," a student suggested from a distance.

A cold current swept though Addy, suddenly trapped in her old self. "I can't deal with this, not right now, with all this," her arm sweeping across the unwelcome audience. "Just leave them there and I'll think about it, not that I want to think about it. I don't know if I want to know what's in there." Addy turned to walk back to her house, looking over her shoulder to the disappointed students and Rio, shrugging his shoulders, dismayed.

***

The sun was setting, the house growing dark. She poured herself two fingers of Scotch, no more, no less, and sat at the kitchen island rubbing her forehead, kicking the stool leg with her heal. Her first reaction was to wonder why they hadn't just opened them and let her know. Why all the drama? What's the big deal about three metal boxes a couple feet under the ground? It's anybody's guess how they got there.

Then she remembered Rio's question about how long she had lived at 85 Iroquois Road, and realized that he must think the previous owners had buried them over thirty years ago. Who were they? It was so long ago, and she had had nothing to do with the purchase. It was her father's doing, his way to get her out of his house. He'd found the house in foreclosure. It was a great deal and perfect for a single woman - a small, two bedroom cape in good shape, sitting above the road, close to the elementary school. At her age it was "beyond time" that she moved out and on, he had said, and all she had to do was take over the mortgage. The mortgagee had died and had no heirs. Her dad knew the broker. It was as good as done.

Addy knew nothing about the previous owner and, moving in, she found the house empty of all evidence of a life. The bank had removed the furniture and personal effects. A few times during her first year, a sales receipt or stray sock or utensil would magically appear behind the hot water heater or washing machine, or at the back of a kitchen cabinet. Not that it mattered. The novelty of living alone and subsequent isolation that first year was all-consuming for a 35 year-old woman, and left no room for innocuous speculation.

Maybe there was information about the previous owner in the bank documents she hadn't looked at since she paid off the mortgage, Addy wondered. Did she even know where they were? She could look for them, but why bother? What difference would it make? It was recent history, not ancient. This "discovery" was overblown by Rio from the beginning. She had the answer: They can just open the damned things if they wanted.

The house was completely dark now. She heard the student's cars start and saw the flash of headlights on her front windows. She knew Rio was always the last to leave for Spectacular, was probably tidying things up under the canopy. Quickly getting up from the island in the dark, she was suddenly light-headed and disoriented. Fearing Rio would be gone before she could tell him, Addy nervously fumbled for the light switch, flicking it on and off a few times to get his attention, bracing herself against the wall to restore her balance.

It worked. He was knocking at the kitchen door, his face in the window. He was not wearing a mask and she didn't care. She was not wearing a mask and he didn't notice. "Are you alright? Is something the matter?" he asked. She heard genuine concern in his voice.

"Can we talk?"

"Can I come in?"

"Please."

***

"I'm having a drink," she said, her equilibrium returning. "I call it 'my restorative.' One a night at this time. I know I shouldn't drink alone. But I do. Care to join me? All I have is scotch."

"Sure," Rio replied with little enthusiasm.

"I guess you must think I'm a little strange and frustrating," she began, handing him exactly two fingers of her favorite. "I don't handle the unexpected very well, do I? I thrive on predictability and crash when surprised. I struggle with making decisions, especially those that affect my life. I

148

live independent of others by necessity, I think, not by choice. I could never accommodate all the questions that accompany close companionship. And at my age, I know myself too well to even consider a life otherwise." Addy paused, realizing this was a description of herself she had never revealed to anyone, amazed that she could put the words together in the moment. "I hope this explains my hesitancy to allow your dig and my reaction this afternoon."

"I get it," Rio said quietly. "It must be hard to rely solely on yourself for everything." He almost added that he thought it abnormal. "Especially under unexpected circumstances."

In the friendly light of the kitchen and soothing glow of her second scotch, relaxed by her confession, Addy felt an unusual attraction for Rio, as if he were a kindred spirit, a confidant, a friend. He'd been growing a beard since arriving, looking more like a professor and archaeologist and it comforted her. "I wanted to catch you before you left tonight to tell you to go ahead and open those things with the kids tomorrow. I don't want to be there. You can just tell me what you find when you leave tomorrow afternoon."

"You're sure you trust us to do this? There could be something very valuable in them. I feel uncomfortable opening them without you present. I'd really rather not."

Addy, having made the decision, when confronted with his rejection, suffered her preservatory instinct to escape the dilemma. "I hate this. Why can't you agree with me, just once?"

Rio ignored the question. "If it's the presence of the students that upset you this afternoon, I have an idea. Why don't we open them right now, right here on your island, together, like we're fellow archaeologists? But casually, drink in hand. What do you think? Just get it over with. We're both making too big a deal of this."

***

Addy looked away from Rio toward the yard where the containers sat in the dark. *Why not get it over with?*, she thought. "Why not?" she said out loud, and poured herself one more finger as he left to fetch them.

***

Rio returned quickly with the containers and his tool belt. Before placing the containers on the island he wiped them clean with a wet paper towel. The process revealed that each had a number scratched into its top, a 1, 2, and 3. "Should we open them in the sequence suggested by the numbers?" Rio asked.

Addy watched in a state of nervous anticipation. "Do you think that's what the numbers mean?"

"Could be. Let's do it in that order." Rio took a pair of needle nose pliers from his tool belt and clawed at the hinges of number 1. Rusted and fragile, they fell away with little effort and he lifted the container top up and over to hang off the latch, reached in and withdrew a clear plastic bag of folded papers. "How're you doing, Addy?" he inquired. "Doesn't look like buried treasure, but could be a map to some. Ready to find out?"

"Sure," Addy said, nodding her head as he spilled the contents onto the island, a disappointing single sheet of folded 81/2 by 11 paper and two keys. "These might be the keys to containers two and three. Maybe this will tell us. Here, you should read this," he said as he handed the document to her.

"Out loud?" she asked.

"If you want. Up to you."

"It's still pretty legible after all these years. Here goes."

***

If you are reading this letter, you have found the grave of my partner Raymond Foster. Please do not dig any deeper.

With the help of Funeral Director Spencer I was allowed to bury Ray on the land we loved so dearly. Very shortly I will be buried six feet adjacent to this site. We are the victims of HIV. You should find two other locked metal boxes beside this one. One holds the paperwork necessary for us to be buried here. The other holds some discoveries we have made in our 12 years on this beautiful mountainside..

Neither of us has a will, being too young to consider the need for one. This plague caught us by surprise. We never imagined our lives would be cut so short. We kept our illness to ourselves for obvious reasons, afraid of the public reaction to the sickness.

We never imagined that we would ever live in a place as magical as this. It was a blessing above all others. These last days for Ray we have listened often to Dylan's song "Time Passes Slowly" as we fought the inevitable. Time does pass slowly up here in the mountains, and we needed all of the time we could get to come to terms with reality. Now Ray is gone, time has no meaning, and I will soon join him.

We decided to leave our most precious belongings to the elemental forces of nature. Please honor the contents of the third box with the significance they deserve. And please leave our graves undisturbed.

Arthur Bettencourt
August 12, 1985

***

"Oh my God, Rio, oh my God," Addy said softly, her hands shaking. "Did you expect something like this? Someone's grave in my backyard?"

"I had no idea."

"What about that whatdayacallit imaging with the drones? You said you saw stuff."

"Not this. We didn't see this"

"What do we do now?"

151

"We open the other two boxes. Look at the paperwork and whatever else they left behind. If the documents are what I think, we must leave the graves undisturbed. Can we open number three next? The letter gives us permission. I'm really curious."

"If you want." Addy was lost in the moment, unable to have an opinion.

Snapping off the hinges, Rio lifted the cover up and over to hang like the first. An opaque plastic bag filled the container and Rio cupped his hands under its bottom to gently remove it to the island. Using his pliers he carefully tore the bag open to reveal two flint arrowheads, a black, shiny, round stone gouge, and a litter of pottery shards embossed with lines and dots in wonderfully mysterious patterns.

Addy, her hands over her cheeks, was amazed. "Oh my, I had no idea. Living here all this time, they were here too, all of them, all along. I was not alone."

J.Michael Wilhelm, EdD.has been a teacher, principal, and school system superintendent for over forty-five years. He has served on Maine's Charter School Commission and is currently a consultant for the Maine Department of Education. He was the 2003 Maine Superintendent of the year. He has published articles in the Maine Journal of Education and Maine Schools in Focus and is the author of A Fork in the Road: Narrative Problem Solving for School Leaders (Rowman and Littlefield, 2018.) He lives in the lake region of Maine with his wife and two dogs.

This collection of short stories are an outgrowth from writing case studies for a book on narrative problem solving for school leaders. I wrote those case studies as short stories with characters and setting to capture the human side of the complicated personnel, student and constituent ssues that arise in school systems. I enjoyed the process so much that after finishing the book I explored writing short stories about other themes and issues.

www.ingramcontent.com/pod-product-compliance
Lightning Source LLC
Chambersburg PA
CBHW050404110726
47899CB00008B/2645